Memory

Previously published as *Secret*

Philippe Grimbert

Translated from the French by Polly McLean

Simon & Schuster
New York   London   Toronto   Sydney

Simon & Schuster
1230 Avenue of the Americas
New York, NY 10020

First Simon & Schuster edition February 2008

SIMON & SCHUSTER and colophon are registered trademarks
of Simon & Schuster, Inc.

For information about special discounts for bulk purchases,
please contact Simon & Schuster Special Sales at
1-800-456-6798 or business@simonandschuster.com.

Manufactured in the United States of America

1   3   5   7   9   10   8   6   4   2

Library of Congress Cataloging-in-Publication Data

Grimbert, Philippe.
[Secret. English]
Memory / Philippe Grimbert ; translated from the French by Polly McLean.
p. cm.
I. McLean, Polly. II. Title.

PQ2667.R493S4313 2008
843'.92—dc22   2007021785

ISBN-13: 978-1-4165-5999-3
ISBN-10: 1-4165-5999-X

To Tania and Maxime,
and to Simon

I

ALTHOUGH AN ONLY child, for many years I had a brother. Holiday friends and casual acquaintances had no option but to take my word for it. I had a brother. Stronger and better looking. An older brother, invisible and glorious.

I always felt envious when I went to stay with a friend and a similar-looking boy walked in. The same disheveled hair and lopsided grin would be introduced with two words: "My brother." An enigma, this intruder with whom everything must be shared, even love. A real brother. Someone in whose face you discovered like features: a persistently straying lock of hair, a pointy tooth . . . A roommate of whom you knew the most intimate things: moods, tastes, weaknesses, smell. Exotic, for me who reigned alone over the empire of my family's four-room flat.

I was the sole object of the love and tender care of my

parents, yet I didn't sleep well, troubled by bad dreams. I would start crying as soon as my light was turned out, not knowing for whom I wept the tears that sank into my pillow and disappeared into the night. Ashamed without understanding why, and often riddled with senseless guilt, I would delay my drift into sleep. As a child, every day provided me with sorrows and fears that I fueled with my solitude. I needed someone with whom to share those tears.

A DAY CAME when I was no longer alone. I had insisted on accompanying my mother to the attic, which she wanted to tidy. I discovered a musty-smelling, unknown room under the rafters, full of rickety furniture and piles of suitcases with rusty locks. She opened a trunk in which she expected to find the fashion magazines that used to publish her designs. She jumped when she saw the little dog with Bakelite eyes, sleeping there on top of a pile of blankets. Threadbare and dusty-muzzled, he was wearing a knitted coat. I immediately grabbed him and hugged him to my chest, but had to abandon the idea of taking him to my room: I could feel my mother's unease as she asked me to put him back in his place.

That night, for the first time, I rubbed my wet cheek against a brother's chest. He had just come into my life; I would take him with me everywhere.

From that day on I walked in his tracks, drowning in his shadow as in an oversize suit. He came with me to the park, to school; I talked about him to everyone I met. At home, I even made up a game to bring him into our lives: I insisted that we wait for him before sitting down at table, that he be served before me, that his bags be packed before mine when we went on holiday. I had created a brother behind whom I could withdraw, a brother who would burden me with the full force of his weight.

ALTHOUGH I HATED my thinness and sickly pallor, I wanted to believe that I was my father's pride and joy. My mother adored me—I was the only one to have lived inside that toned belly, to have appeared from between those athletic thighs. I was the first, the only one. Before me, nobody. Just a night, some shadowy memories, and a few black-and-white photographs celebrating the meeting of two superb bodies, fit from athletic discipline, who would unite their paths to give me life, love me, and lie to me.

According to them, I had always had this very French surname. My origins didn't condemn me to certain death; I was no longer a spindly branch at the top of a family tree in need of pollarding.

My christening took place so late that I could still

remember it all: the gestures of the officiating priest, the damp cross imprinted on my forehead, and leaving the church held close under the embroidered wing of his stole. A bastion between me and divine wrath. If by misfortune its thunder should rage once more, my name on the sacristy register would protect me. I didn't know what was going on and joined in the game obediently, silently, trying to believe—along with everyone present— that we were merely making up for a simple oversight.

The indelible cut to my penis became nothing more than the reminder of a necessary surgical intervention. Not a ritual but a medical decision, one among many. Our surname too was scarred: my father had arranged for two letters to be changed by deed poll, creating a different spelling that allowed him to plant roots deep in French soil.

The destructive mission undertaken by killers a few years before my birth thus continued underground, spreading secrets and silences, cultivating shame, mutilating names, and engendering lies. In defeat, the persecutor continued to triumph.

Despite these precautions the truth bubbled to the surface, thanks to certain details: a few slices of unleavened bread dipped in egg and fried until golden; a modern-style samovar on the living room mantelpiece; a candlestick locked into the cupboard beneath the dresser. And the constant questions: people were always asking me about the origins of the name Grimbert, wondering how exactly it was spelled, unearthing the *n* that an *m* had replaced, flushing out the *g* that a *t* was supposed to efface from memory. I brought these questions home; they were brushed aside by my father. We've always had that name, he would snap. That much was obvious and not to be contradicted: our name could be traced right back to the Middle Ages—wasn't Grimbert a hero of the *Roman de Renart*? An *m* for an *n,* a *t* for a *g;* two tiny changes. But of course *M* for mute hid the *N* of Nazism, while *G* for ghosts vanished under taciturn *T*.

I was constantly bashing up against the painful wall with which my parents had surrounded themselves, but loved them too much to try to climb it, reopening the wound. I had decided not to know.

FOR A LONG time my brother helped me surmount my fears. A squeeze of his hand on my arm, his fingers ruffling my hair, and I would find the strength to overcome obstacles. Sitting at a school desk, his shoulder against mine provided reassurance, and often when I was asked a question, his voice whispered the correct answer into my ear.

He displayed the pride of rebels doing exactly as they pleased, playground champions jumping for balls, heroes climbing the railings. I admired them, my back against the wall, incapable of competing, praying for the liberating bell so I could finally get back to my books. I had chosen myself a triumphant brother. Unbeatable, he won everything while I paraded my fragility before my father, trying not to see the disappointment flickering in his eyes.

MY PARENTS, MY dear parents, whose every muscle had been buffed and toned, like those statues in the galleries of the Louvre that I found so unsettling. High-board diving and gymnastics for my mother, wrestling and apparatus work for my father, tennis and volleyball for the two of them; their bodies made to meet, marry, and reproduce.

I was the fruit of this union, but would stand in front of the mirror with morbid pleasure, enumerating my imperfections: bony knees, pelvis showing through the skin, gangly arms. How frightening I found that hollow beneath my solar plexus, about the size of a fist, gouging out my chest like the permanent mark of a blow.

Doctors' surgeries, dispensaries, hospitals. The smell of disinfectant barely covering the sour sweat of fear. A noxious environment to which I added my own contribution, coughing under the stethoscope, stretching out my arm for the needle. Every week my mother took me to one of these now familiar places, helping me undress to display my symptoms to a specialist who would then take her away for a private, whispered conversation. Resigned, I remained on the examination table awaiting a verdict: some kind of intervention no doubt, or long-term treatment—at the very best vitamins or inhalations. Years spent treating this faltering body. Meanwhile my brother brazenly showed off his broad shoulders and suntanned skin covered in downy blond hair.

Chinning bar, weights bench, wall bars . . . my father trained every day in a room of our flat, which they'd converted into a gym. Although my mother spent less time in there, she did use it for warm-up exercises, watching for the slightest slackening so she could remedy it immediately.

The two of them ran a wholesale business on the rue du Bourg-l'Abbé, in an area specializing in hosiery, in one of the oldest neighborhoods of Paris. Most of the sports shops bought their swimsuits, leotards, and underwear from my parents. I would stand at the till with my mother, greeting the clients. Sometimes I would help my father, trotting behind him into one or other of the storerooms to watch him effortlessly pick up stacks of boxes adorned with photos of sportsmen and -women—gymnasts on the rings, swimmers, javelin throwers—which he would then pile onto the shelves. The men had the same short, slightly wavy hair as my father; the women shared my mother's dark cascade, tied back with a ribbon.

SOON AFTER MY discovery in the attic I had insisted on going back up there, and this time my mother couldn't stop me bringing the little dog down with me. I moved him on to my bed that very evening.

Whenever I fell out with my brother I took refuge in my new friend, Si. Where did I get that name? From the dusty smell of his fur? The silences of my mother, my father's sadness? Si, Si! I walked my dog all around the flat, not wanting to notice my parents' distress when they heard me calling his name.

The older I got, the more tense my relationship with my brother became. I invented quarrels and rebelled against his authority. I tried to make him yield, but I rarely came out the winner.

★ ★ ★

He had changed over the years. From protective, he had become tyrannical, mocking, even contemptuous. I nevertheless continued to tell him my fears and failings as I fell asleep to the rhythm of his breathing. He received them without a word, but his gaze reduced me to nothing; he would examine my imperfections, lifting the sheets and stifling a laugh. Then anger would overwhelm me, and I'd seize him by the throat. Enemy brother, false brother, ghost brother, return to your night! Fingers in his eyes, I would push down on his face as hard as I could, trying to force him into the shifting sands of the pillow.

He laughed, and the two of us rolled around under the covers, reinventing crazy games in the half-light of our bedroom. Unsettled by his touch, I imagined the softness of his skin.

MY BONES LENGTHENED, drawing attention to my skin-niness. The school doctor noticed and summoned my parents to check that I was getting enough to eat. They came back distressed. Though I was angry with myself for making them feel ashamed, in my eyes their glamour was only reinforced: I hated my body, and my admiration for theirs now knew no bounds. I was discovering a new way to take pleasure in my loser status: lack of sleep hollowed out my cheeks a little more each day, the startling good health of my parents contrasting ever more with my sickly appearance.

My face had the pallor and bluish rings under the eyes of a child exhausted by solo activities. Whenever I shut myself in my room I took with me the image of a body, the warmth of flesh. When I wasn't entangling my limbs with those of my brother, I cherished the thunderbolt that jolted through me every break time; in the playground I used to take refuge on the edge of the girls' area—they played hopscotch and skipping rope there, far from the ball games and shouts that rang out on the boys' territory. Sitting on the cement floor close to their high voices, I let myself be soothed by their laughs and rhymes, and when they jumped, caught a glimpse of white knickers under skirts.

My curiosity about bodies was limitless. Very soon the shield of clothing ceased to hide anything from me; my eyes were like those magic glasses I had seen advertised in a magazine, claiming to be as strong as X rays. Released from their town clothes, passersby revealed both their treasures and their failings. I barely had to glance to notice a crooked leg, a perky pair of breasts, or a protuberant belly. My trained eye gathered a veritable harvest of images, a collection of bodies that I pored over when night came.

In the rue du Bourg-l'Abbé, I made the most of days when my parents were busy to explore the stock. The shop was on the ground floor of a dilapidated building. A staircase led up to what had been a flat; the dark rooms were lined with shelving and suffused with the smell of cardboard and paint. Just as I might have scoured library shelves for a particular book, I let my gaze run along the labels: swimming costumes, sports knickers, footless tights. Small, medium, large, girl, woman; I compared them all, taking note of the sizes, each number making me imagine a new body suddenly clothed in these items. When I was sure I wouldn't be disturbed I opened the boxes, heart beating wildly, and grabbed the contents. I sank my face into them, and then laid them out on the counter while pressing my stomach up against the oak trim, trying in my own way to re-create the pose of a gymnast, basketball player, or long-distance runner.

THE SHOP SHARED the ground floor of the building with the consulting rooms of Mademoiselle Louise. Her domain consisted of two rooms: an office and a treatment room, both painted glossy white with linoleum floors. A few sickly plants dressed a window on which enamel letters described the services available: home treatments, injections, massages. Louise was family; I had always known her. On quiet days she would come and lean on the counter to have a chat. She regularly massaged my parents on a table covered with a white sheet, and once a week injected me with vitamins or sat me down in front of her aerosol pump: I would sit quite still as the nozzles spluttered up into my nostrils, plunged in thought, made drowsy by the humming of the machine.

Louise was in her sixties. Her face bore the scars of alcohol and tobacco; years of excess had given her permanent bags under the eyes, and her pale skin floated loosely on a ruined face. Only her vigorous hands, emerging from the sleeves of her white coat, seemed to have bone structure: two authoritative hands, with short nails and long fingers that fluttered and asserted themselves as she spoke. I enjoyed her company, and would cross the narrow, box-filled corridor as often as possible to visit her. I spent less time at the shop than at her place, where I could talk freely. I felt close to her, probably because of her lopsided walk—the result of a clubfoot hidden in an orthopedic shoe: a black leather ball and chain that she dragged with her everywhere. Her unsteady body bumping into the corridor walls seemed an echo of her face, a sack of skin unsupported by any framework. Prone to rheumatic episodes that inflamed her joints, Louise waved the dull pain away with an exasperated flick of her hand. I understood why: she hated the way she looked.

I was fascinated by her boneless body, so intimate with our own: those of my parents, who regularly dumped their tiredness on her massage table, and mine too, when I turned my naked buttocks to her so she could inject one of her regenerative potions.

LOUISE SAID SHE'D known my parents since they moved to the rue du Bourg-l'Abbé. She would rave about my mother's beauty and my father's stylishness, quivering as she said their surname.

We had our rituals. Whenever I dropped by she made me a hot chocolate on the little stove she used for boiling her needles. I sipped it slowly, and she kept me company with a glass of the amber liqueur she hid in her medicine cabinet. I was curious about her life, and asked her the questions I'd never allowed myself to ask my parents. She claimed she had no secrets—this was her life, in these gloomy rooms, treating her regulars, listening to them day after day. The rest was so uninteresting: she lived in the house she'd been born and grown up in—her horizons extended no farther than the two consulting rooms and the limestone house with its small suburban garden. Since her father's death she had cared for her mother there, spending her evenings treating the frail old woman in much the same way she looked after clients during the daytime.

On days more favorable to the telling of secrets, Louise talked of having been mocked for her limp as a young girl, and living in the shadow of her more agile friends. I could relate to that. I wanted to know more, but almost immediately—as with every time she spoke about something difficult—Louise did that same thing to get rid of the pain: she swept the air with her hands and looked questioningly into my eyes, waiting for me to confide in her. Which gave me license to tell her my dreams. These tales of mine were punctuated by my sighs, made visible by the smoke of her cigarette.

For years she had been listening to my parents with the same attention, letting her strong hands run over them and rid them of their worries: along with their tiredness, they deposited their secrets with her.

II

FOR A LONG time I was a young boy who dreamed of having a perfect family. I used the rare glimpses they gave me to build a picture of how my parents had met. A few incidental words about their childhood, snippets of information about their youth, their love . . . I pounced on these fragments to create my unlikely tale. In my own way I unwound the tangle of their lives and, much as I had invented myself a brother, created from scratch the meeting of the two bodies from which I was born, as if I were writing a novel.

Sport was the passion that brought Maxime and Tania together: where else could my story start but at the sports club I visited with them so often?

The grounds, pool, and gyms of the Alsace Sports Club run alongside the Marne. If you drive along the riverbank scattered with open-air cafés you come to a gate with a metal stork perched on top. On Sundays people flock to dance at these *guinguettes* and eat fried fish, washed down with rather tart white wine, at the adjoining restaurants. Boys in shirtsleeves and girls in flowered dresses dance close to the sound of an accordion, and in the height of summer peel off their clothes to dive into the cool water. The carefree bathers and noisy dancers contrast with the deep breaths and sighs of the spartans in white shorts, training with ostentatious discipline on the lawns of the club.

Maxime is the prince of this tribe. He shines in the gym, floors his opponents in Greco-Roman wrestling, and effortlessly holds a crucifix position on the rings. He has something to prove, having started work very young in his father's hosiery and sportswear business. The meager resources of Joseph, a Romanian immigrant, meant that his three children couldn't stay in school very long. The two eldest resigned themselves to their fate, marrying young and placidly repeating their father's life. But Maxime would have liked to become a doctor or lawyer, one of those careers that come with a title. Being a Dr. or Juris Dr. would have helped people forget the foreign sound of his surname. One senses in that name a certain uprooting, a temptation to roll one's *r*'s, a hint of central European cooking—remnants too pronounced for this young man desperate to be fashionable and stylish. He is in love with Paris, wants to melt into it, adopt its trends, be filled with its carefree fragrance.

Maxime—the favorite of his mother, Caroline, who died when he was still a child—loves to seduce. He dresses well, wears tailor-made shirts. He likes to stand out, and his first major purchase is a convertible with leather seats and polished chrome. He cruises around Paris on the lookout for women, elbow resting on the open window, hair blown back by the wind, slowing alongside taxi stands to offer a lift to some unknown girl. He quickly gets used to seeing his charm reflected in the eyes of the young women.

Driving along the banks of the Marne one day, he notices the sports club gates. Impressed by the zeal of the young men and women, he joins immediately, and starts to practice different sports in a quest for the perfect body.

In a few years, weights and apparatus work have given him the body of his dreams: his athletic build belies his origins.

TANIA IS THE only one to notice the invisible lines making up the sports grounds. Her artist's eye uses them to create abstractions: steel rails, sparks, tensions, and slackenings that she transforms into splashes of color in her sketchbook.

She works as a catwalk model, and the rest of the time sketches figures that she sells to a fashion magazine. Three-quarter portraits of women, swaying slightly, dressed in printed materials and with feathers in their hair. She lives in the rue Berthe at the foot of Montmartre, in the two-bedroom flat adjoining her mother's dressmaking studio. As a little girl she used to sit on a stool for hours watching the fluttering hands of this plump woman, wearing a smock and slippers, creating miracles of elegance. Being around her mother's designs refined her childhood drawings until she was filling whole notebooks, creating figures with wide

28

shoulders and narrow waists. She left school as soon as she had her primary school certificate and enrolled in a dress-designing course, having attracted attention with the skill of her drawing.

The two women live alone. Martha makes clothes day and night to provide her daughter with a comfortable life. Tania's father has abandoned them. Tania keeps a photo of him on her bedside table, a bow in his hand and his gaunt face transformed by the photographer's skill into that of a mysterious virtuoso. He has passed on to her an English-sounding surname, beyond reproach. Martha's surname carries the vestiges of her immigrant ancestors, of Lithuania, a Russian province of indistinct borders that Tania would struggle to find on a map.

André was an unemployed violinist who earned money from occasional work, playing "Black Eyes" or "Kalinka" in the capital's Russian cabarets, or accompanying variety-show singers in down-market music halls. Tania was tiny when he started trying to teach her his instrument; she retains a terrified memory of those lessons. She would have loved to satisfy his paternal ambition by being one of those child prodigies with their photo in the newspaper, but the instrument would yield only unbearable screeching, piercing her father's eardrums and unleashing his fury.

One day André left the rue Berthe without warning; they never saw him again. The most recent news they had received was scribbled on the back of postcards sent from Africa. What was he doing there? Tania imagined her father in some bush village teaching violin to native children far more gifted than herself.

This abandonment has left her full of nostalgia for an artistic career. Tania knows she is beautiful, but neither compliments nor the eloquent gazes of passersby are enough to reassure her. As a schoolgirl she suffered from her lack of brilliance: with the exception of drawing, only her physical attributes were noted. One of her friends who trained at the Alsace suggested she come along, and very soon Tania excelled there.

MAXIME HAS NOTICED Tania's beauty; he wants her. Tania too is attracted by this boy. She looks out for his arrival, follows him with her eyes, and occasionally drops in at the gym to watch one of his matches. The sight of Maxime in his wrestling gear pinning an opponent in the stranglehold of his legs leaves her far from indifferent.

Tania is utterly gorgeous in her tight black swimsuit and a white cap that emphasizes the purity of her features. A couple of bounces project her up toward the sky; she slices through space and then folds into herself to create perfect shapes in the air before zooming toward the water, which closes around her with barely a splash. Maxime always makes sure to be at the foot of the diving board when the women's team is training.

He likes an easy conquest. Sets his heart on a dainty

ankle, a cleavage shimmering in the summer sun. A smile, a lingering look, and the young prey slides into his convertible. He takes her out to dinner, looks at her with a gaze full of promise. Set ablaze by the moment, dazzled by a detail, he confuses desire with love and very soon the delight of the encounter fades.

He can already tell it won't be like that with Tania. Unusually for him, he decides not to rush. His practiced eye is used to pitilessly pinpointing the weak spot in any body, however promising it may seem. A leg not shapely enough, a foot too square, a hint of softness in the belly and suddenly the charm of a pretty chest or lower back vanishes. Nothing of the sort with Tania: everything about her body provokes his desire.

As they get to know each other, the invulnerable champion gradually reveals some fragility and doubts. He glimpses the little girl peeping from behind the statue. After a few weeks he can't bear to be apart from her. They meet outside the club, he takes her in his convertible to see his favorite parts of the capital: the Concorde in the rain, the provincial charm of the Place Furstenberg, the Aligre market, the little country cemetery surrounding the church at Charonne.

A FEW MONTHS later they move into this quiet neighborhood, into the flat where I will be born. The following year they decide to get married. Tania stops modeling and joins Maxime in the shop in the rue du Bourg-l'Abbé; under their management the business begins to specialize in sportswear.

Maxime is still full of wonder at their meeting. Tania feels this richness too, but she would like a child. Maxime hesitates—he wants Tania to himself for a few more years. The increasing threat of the war gives him a further justification: is it right to create new life in these troubled times?

Paris is waiting. One can feel it in the agitation of the streets, in the debates raging near the newspaper stands. Maxime and Tania are working harder than ever; the shop is more and more busy, as if the threat of catastrophe is provoking a fever of spending. This atmosphere can also be felt at the club, where they continue to train. Everyone is trying to outdo themselves; matches are increasing in intensity, throwing opponents into ever more fierce sparring, in thrall to a growing thirst for victory.

They learn of the invasion of Poland by German troops. Radio broadcasts are often alarming—Maxime and Tania listen to them huddled around the big walnut radio set in the small makeshift office above the shop.

On the front pages of newspapers, black letters resembling death notices announce the declaration of war. It feels unreal to them: two armies, obeying incomprehensible political strategies developed in distant offices, about to go into battle to the north of France along intangible borders. They will hear no explosions, no cries of agony. France, well sheltered behind the Maginot line—whose invulnerability has so often been vaunted—will quickly emerge victorious. To their eyes, that which will be played out in mud and blood seems almost like a sporting competition.

EVERY TIME MY parents talked about the war years, they mentioned the village that took them in when penury and the threat of forced conscription drove them across the demarcation line. They had closed the shop and given the keys to Louise, their neighbor and faithful friend. She would make sure their stock remained safe while they were away. One of her cousins, who worked for a town council in the Indre, had given them the address of a family likely to put them up. Confident of finding shelter, they left Paris for Saint-Gaultier, whose name they always spoke with elation. They associated it with two extraordinary years, a time of great happiness, a serene oasis in the storm.

They find refuge in the house of a retired colonel who lives with his daughter, herself an elderly lady who used to be a teacher. The small town is an island of tranquillity, far from the rumblings of war. The anxieties, hardships, and rationings suffered in the cities don't seem to have reached it. The colonel has good relationships with the nearby farmers, whom he has known for a long time. Since the beginning of the hostilities these farmers have been slaughtering livestock on the quiet; meat and basic food-stuffs are not lacking. For the first few days Maxime and Tania cannot believe their eyes as fresh eggs, butter, and roasted meat appear on the colonel's table.

They live in a garret and share the quiet life of their hosts, whose evenings are punctuated by the chiming of a wall clock. Maxime earns his board and lodging by working in the grounds of the estate and of neighboring properties, splitting logs for winter and tending the flower beds and vegetable gardens. Tania teaches the local school-children gymnastics. These activities leave them enough time to explore the area, cycling around the steep roads that climb the nearby hills. When it's sunny enough, Tania swims across the Creuse; sometimes she climbs onto the pier of a ruined, current-dashed bridge and dives into the cool water. Maxime sits on the grassy bank gazing at her body haloed by the sun.

In the evenings, after spending time with the colonel and his daughter, Maxime and Tania leave the grounds just as the small town beds down for the night. They walk along the dusky riverbanks and kiss like young lovers, leaning against the still-warm stone walls that run alongside the path. The lapping of the river emphasizes the tranquillity of the place; ghostly moonlight shines over the city walls looming above them. How to imagine screaming sirens dragging terrified families from their sleep? How to conceive the horror and fear of women and children huddled against one another in the half-light of cellars that may become their graves?

As the cool of the night falls on their shoulders they return to the house, squeezing each other tight, making sure the oak boards don't creak as they climb the stairs, and love each other silently in the narrow bed, intertwined until dawn.

FOR SO LONG I thought I was the first, the only one. I would like to have been born from my parents' loving at Saint-Gaultier, in the little room under the rafters, when they came back from their nocturnal strolls. Less afflicted than others by the war, the humiliations and crimes of the invaders, they thought of those years as an extended holiday. I imagined a kindly point man sending the long convoy of bereavements, suffering, and horrors on a special detour around Saint-Gaultier, so that its evil freight didn't pass through the peaceful streets of the little town. The war, reduced to news broadcast by the nasal voices of reporters, exhibited its horrors only on the radio; the terrifying images would be kept for the history books.

On their return to Paris, Maxime and Tania found the shop intact but were vexed to note the wealth of the neighboring shopkeepers. Those who hadn't been forced to flee had built substantial fortunes, thanks to the paucity of competition and the extraordinary rise in prices. Louise had waited for them, watching over their goods as if they were her own. She had survived the ordeals and humiliations.

The early postwar years are less comfortable than those of their retreat in the Indre—it is difficult to find supplies; goods are only trickling through; industries need time to get back on their feet. The weaving looms in the Aube valley are turning day and night, the factories are struggling to meet their order books. Maxime and Tania's table is not exactly laden with food; rationing is still in effect. Nevertheless, they take up their old habits, clients flock back to the shop, and the two of them return to the banks of the Marne to devote themselves to their training once more.

A few years later, the country's scars seem to have healed over. Tania once again puts pressure on Maxime; she has wanted this child for so long. But he is still reluctant. Their life together fills him with such joy, his desire for Tania is as strong as ever, and the same old hesitations hold him back. He doesn't want to share his wife. Later he'll say, talking about my conception, smiling, that this child slipped out of him.

When she finally falls pregnant, Tania watches with delight as her belly grows round. But as soon as she goes into labor there are complications. There is talk of forceps, even a cesarean. Eventually the fruit of the union of these two athletes is there, wrapped in a cloth: very different from what they had dreamed of, a delicate child they must keep from the jaws of death.

I survived, thanks to the care of the doctors and the love of my mother. I would like to think that my father loved me too—overcoming his disappointment and finding in care, worry, and protectiveness enough to stoke his feelings. But his first look left its trace on me, and I regularly glimpsed that flash of bitterness in his eyes.

III

AT THE BEGINNING of each year I set myself the same goal: to attract the attention of my teachers, become their favorite, and be called to the podium. This was the only competition I could possibly win. It was my field—the rest of the world I had abandoned to my brother: only he could conquer it.

The smell of new books intoxicated me. I got drunk on the almond fragrance of book glue, on the leather of the satchel, in which I buried my face. Exercise books accumulated in my desk drawers; I never reread them. The vigor I lacked for physical activities became incandescent when, pen in hand, I filled whole pages with invented stories. Sometimes they were intimately about me—family tales, parental exploits—sometimes they became horrific stories sprinkled with torture, death, and reunion: crazy games and tear-soaked sagas.

The years passed, and I gradually and effortlessly surmounted the challenges of each class. At school as at home I was the model child. My mother took me to the Louvre once a week, my father shared with me his passion for Paris—we would go around together looking for places undiscovered by tourists. My world was restricted to the three of us. On Sundays my parents met up with their sporty friends for volleyball or tennis matches. Sitting on the grass with my pen and notebook, I feasted my eyes on these leaping bodies glistening with sweat in the sun, enriching my collection of images. I never took part in the games played by the other children, who were already following in their parents' footsteps. I left it to my brother to hang out with them, to fight over the ball and triumph on the tracks and courts left vacant by the adults.

MY PATERNAL GRANDFATHER, Joseph, rang our doorbell every Tuesday, with a jar of Malossol gherkins or a box of Turkish delight in his bag. Sometimes he'd bring me a little parcel full of dried fruits and almonds, inside which was a visual puzzle: you were supposed to find in an idyllic scene the wolf in the middle of a jumble of branches, or the face of the farmer's wife in the cracks of a wall. In his quiet, toneless voice he told me sepia-colored memories. He was unstoppable about Paris during the Belle Epoque but wouldn't say anything about his own childhood. He never said a word about his decision to leave the country in which he was born. He had drawn a line under those years, leaving in his Bucharest suburb the memories of a family he claimed never to have heard from again.

★   ★   ★

On Sunday evenings we ate at George and Esther's. My uncle, who had taken refuge in silence, had no interest in anything but spiritual contemplation. My aunt was a short redhead with a wide mouth and green eyes, which she still emphasized with thick kohl. She livened up those dinners with her incessant chat. In her heyday she must have looked like Sarah Bernhardt; she still had a theatricality about her, and used to faint if squashed in the crowd on market days. Having long lost any hope of dialogue with her husband, she made up for it on Sunday evenings with her in-laws, regaling us with her stories. The rest of the time she chain-smoked and waited for customers in their drapery shop near the Charonne metro station.

Aunt Elise and her husband, Marcel, sold work uniforms—overalls, checked woollen shirts, and dark gray smocks—in the heart of the working-class suburb of Malakoff. Elise read a lot; she would quote famous authors and poets during the weekly meal, and fiercely defend her Marxist beliefs.

I sometimes used to spend short holidays in the nearby suburb where Martha lived. She was plump, fond of food, and eager to please me, and her eyes sparkled behind the thick lenses of her glasses. For a long time I imagined all the grandmothers of all the children in the city living in her street, all welcoming their grandchildren with the same homemade treats, all wearing the same aprons and with the same pretty, puffy hairdos.

Louise was always my favorite, even though she wasn't actually part of the family. Perhaps I felt a deeper complicity with her than with my blood relatives. Affectionate as they were, my uncles, aunts, and grandparents seemed surrounded by an intangible barrier forbidding questions and warding off confidences. A secret club, bound together by an impossible grief.

DURING THE AFTERNOONS we spent together in her dimly lit consulting rooms, Louise slowly spelled out the realities of a war that had come to a close a few years before I was born. She talked and talked: the anguish and humiliation of those who were persecuted must never be forgotten. For a long time, she hid the fact of her personal experience. Until I was fifteen years old, Louise respected the secret in which my parents had shrouded me, the secret that also concerned her. Perhaps she was waiting for a sign before revealing anything further, a word or allusion from me that would give her permission to nudge open the door.

One night there was a film about those years on the television. My father shut himself away in his gym, incapable of watching. The thud of his dumbbells and rasping of his breath blocked out the orders barked in a language he could no longer bear to hear. I remained on the living room sofa, alone with my mother. She was even more silent than usual; of whom was she thinking? Wordlessly, we watched this fiction in black-and-white: studio-reconstructed sets, actors wearing uniforms, extras herded into pens. I was fascinated by the sight of those naked bodies crushed up against one another, couldn't take my eyes off the women covering their breasts, the men with hands cupped over their genitals, walking in single file through the cold on their way to the shower block. The first naked bodies I had ever seen on screen, pale forms standing out against the gray background of the long low buildings. I let my eyes linger on their already defiled flesh, knowing only too well what I would do as soon as I was alone in my room.

I HAD LEFT primary school and was attending the local secondary. I made a point of staying ahead, crossing the finishing line in the top few. Excused from sports for medical reasons, I spent those sessions in the study room immersed in my books. Through the window I could see the others scrapping, trying to grab the ball that rolled among their legs; I could hear their shouts and cheers when a goal was scored. They were as strong and as merciless as my brother, bringing down their opponents as I bent my hollow chest over the desk.

The days went by, each like the last. Night after night, I deployed my cast of ghosts. A perfectly ordered existence, until the event that would change everything.

I HAD GROWN taller, and kept my thin legs and skinny body hidden in baggy clothes. The previous evening I had celebrated my fifteenth birthday. Another anniversary was approaching: the 1945 victory. The headmaster had decided to show his students a documentary. He had us all sit in a darkened classroom facing a sheet stretched over the blackboard. I found myself next to the captain of the football team, a stocky, rowdy, crew-cut boy who had never said a single word to me.

The film began. For the first time I saw the mountains. Those terrible mountains I had only read about. The reels turned, unwinding the film; the only sound was the whirr of the projector. Slagheaps of shoes, of clothes, great piles of hair and body parts. These weren't extras, or sets, in contrast to the film my mother and I had watched in silence. I would have preferred to lock myself away than look at those images. One of them had me pinned to my seat: a uniformed soldier dragging a woman by one foot and hurling her into an already overflowing pit. That broken body had been a woman. A woman who had gone shopping for clothes, who had admired the elegant lines of her new dress in the mirror. A woman who'd tucked a stray lock of hair back into her bun. Now she was just this broken doll, dragged along like a sack, her back bouncing on the pebbles of the path.

The sight was too intense, the obscenity too violent for me to consider taking it back to my bedroom. Even though some nights, with other images, I hadn't hesitated—for example after the TV drama, when I made my choice from among the line of stripped bodies, designating the one I would be submitting to my desires.

My neighbor, the team captain, had been fidgeting around on the bench since the beginning of the screening; taking advantage of the darkness, he had muttered a few coarse remarks that made everyone laugh. He stifled a guffaw when he saw the obscene body, thighs opening on a black triangle every time it juddered. He elbowed me in the ribs and I heard myself laugh too, to please him. I wished I could think of something funny to say, to make him laugh. He imitated a German accent, saying: "Ach! Jewish dogs!" and I laughed again, louder. I laughed because he'd elbowed me, because it was the first time one of those glorious bodies was seeking my complicity. I laughed until I felt sick. Suddenly my stomach lurched; I thought I was going to throw up, and before I knew what I was doing I had slapped him hard across the face. For a moment he was stunned; I just had time to see the black-and-white woman reflected in his staring eyes and then he threw himself on me and started punching me. We rolled under the table. I was no longer myself; for the first time I was fearless, not afraid that his fist was about to fill the hollow of my chest. The nausea had disappeared. I grabbed him by the hair and banged his head against the ground, stuck my fingers in his eyes, spat in his mouth. I wasn't at school, I was struggling as I did every night, with the same fervor. But unlike with my brother, this opponent wasn't going to get the better of me. I knew I would kill him. I was actually going to make his face disappear into those shifting sands.

Alerted by our shouts, the supervisor stopped the film and switched the lights back on. With the help of a few pupils he separated us: I could see only out of one eye and a hot liquid was running down my cheek. I was taken to the first-aid room. My neighbor, whose face was all bloody, was still yelling insults as I left the class. But I had managed to damage his nose quite seriously, which earned me the respect of my classmates for a few weeks.

The incident left me with a plaster above one eye that I wore around school with great pride. But the injury brought me much more than ephemeral glory—it was the sign for which Louise had been waiting.

I TOLD MY old friend everything the next day in the rue du Bourg-l'Abbé. I had given my parents a version that avoided mention of the documentary: a playground scrap because the pen I'd received for my birthday the day before had been pinched. I glimpsed astonishment in my father's eyes, mixed with a touch of satisfaction: could his son actually fight?

To Louise I told the truth. She was the only one I could tell. I told her about the film, about the mountains; I described the rubberlike woman and how I'd avenged the insult done to her. But I didn't mention my laughter. I was telling my story when suddenly, overwhelmed by emotion, I wept in front of Louise as I'd never done with anyone. Her face crumpled; she held me in her arms and I totally let myself go, my cheek against her white nylon coat. I soon felt tears dropping on my forehead. Surprised, I raised my head to see Louise crying too, unrestrainedly. She held me away from herself to look at me, as if wondering what to do. Then she smiled and started to talk.

The day after my fifteenth birthday, I finally learned what I had always known. I too could have stitched the badge to my clothing like my old friend, could have fled persecution like my parents, my beloved statues. Like everyone in my family. Like their fellows—neighbors and strangers —all exposed by the last syllable of their names: *sky, thal, stein* . . . I discovered how those who'd hidden it from me were themselves marked by that terribly burdensome, guilty adjective. Louise was no longer telling me about an anonymous mass of victims but about herself, her tortured body, scarred during the war by a new singularity: that badge, so heavy it emphasized her limping walk. She told me of the words that wounded her, the humiliating notices, the closed doors, the forbidden seats. Her surprise, when it became compulsory to wear the star, at the true identity of some of her neighbors: the grocer at the end of the street, with his very French surname; the retired couple next door; the neighborhood doctor; even the unpleasant pharmacist whom she had thought anti-Semitic. The yellow stain distinguished them to others but also allowed them to recognize one another, binding together a community that, because it was hiding itself, had sometimes not realized its own existence.

I was fifteen years old and this new situation changed the whole thread of my tale. What to do with this adjective, inseparable from my emaciated body so reminiscent of those I had seen floating in too-big pajama uniforms? How to write it in my notebooks? With or without a capital? A new term had just been added to my list. I was no longer merely weak, incapable, inept. Barely had the news fallen from Louise's lips than my new identity started changing me. I was still the same boy but also someone new, someone mysteriously stronger.

So it was neither hardship nor the threat of conscription that had driven my parents to abandon everything and seek refuge in the other half of France. Did Louise really stay in the rue du Bourg-l'Abbé to look after the shop, as they had claimed, or did she leave with them? Was their stay in the Indre really the paradise they had described? I had so many questions to ask, questions that had never yet passed my lips.

Louise was faltering. She had said too much, but she couldn't stop there. She owed me the truth. She was going to break her oath, to betray my parents' confidence for the first time. She loved me enough to do that, she who had never had children of her own or, according to her, experienced romantic love. The elderly spinster saw it as her duty to break the silence for this boy so like herself, marked as she was by his difference. I would no longer believe I was the first, or the only one.

THE MORE LOUISE told me, the more my certainties collapsed. Too much emotion on my part would have cramped her style, so I listened intently, dry-eyed, controlling my reactions. My parents' story, which in my first tale I had imagined so straightforward, became tortuous. Blindly I followed its path, on an exodus that took me away from those I loved toward unfamiliar faces. I walked a road full of murmurs, now able to make out the corpses laid out on the verge.

Three dead people loomed out of the shadows. I heard their names for the first time: Robert, Hannah, and Simon. Robert, Tania's husband. Simon, the son of Maxime and Hannah. I heard Louise say "Tania's husband" and "Maxime's son" and I didn't feel a thing. I learned that before becoming husband and wife, my father and mother had been

brother- and sister-in-law, and I didn't react. I was balancing on the tightrope Louise had just strung out, my hands
gripping the balancing pole, looking far ahead, my eyes
fixed on the end of her tale.

Louise had just said Simon's name, at last. He was
making his first official appearance, having already crept
into all those images, those nameless wrestlers and brutal
boys, those playground tyrants. The brother I had invented,
who had put an end to my solitude, this ghostly big
brother had actually existed. Louise had known him, loved
him. Before he was my grandfather, Joseph had been his.
George, Esther, Marcel, and Elise had been his family.
Before becoming my mother, Tania had been his aunt.
What did he call her, how did she hug him?

After she had described the forbidden places, derogatory
signs, and embroidered stars of the three letters that now
referred to me, Louise wanted to tell me one more thing,
the most painful. But her voice caught in her throat.

I WAS SOON going to have to cross the corridor and walk back into the busy shop. I was no longer the same, and the people I would find there, a few feet from Louise's rooms, were also transformed. Behind the recently removed masks were two lives of unsuspected suffering. My parents noticed my pallor and asked if I was all right. I reassured them with a smile. I watched them; they hadn't changed. The silence was going to continue, and I couldn't imagine what might make me decide to break it. I was trying, in my turn, to protect them.

Over the next few weeks I would visit Louise more often than ever, pressing forward with my inquiry. My friend steadily opened new chapters, making the events I'd learned about in history books—the Occupation, Vichy, the fate of the Jews, the demarcation line—no longer mere

61

titles in a school textbook. They had suddenly come to life, like black-and-white photos restored to color. My parents had lived these events, been affected by them much more than I had realized.

Hannah appeared out of nowhere: Maxime's first wife, with her pale eyes and porcelain skin. An anxious, tender mother devoted to her only son. More a mother than a wife, Louise would say, in order to excuse Maxime and avoid condemning Tania.

I made Simon's acquaintance—his father's pride and his mother's delight, with the makings of a champion, agile and commanding almost as soon as he could walk. When Louise's voice faltered, I remained untouched: I couldn't seem to feel pity. Everything she told me about Simon provoked a dull anger of which I already felt ashamed. I tried to imagine his suffering, his body grown thin as mine, shivering in coarse fabric, his ribs sticking out, his childhood reduced to a handful of ashes in the Polish wind. But I felt the fierce bite of jealousy when Louise described his features and his beautifully formed body, a carbon copy of Maxime, looked upon admiringly by him.

Having lived all these years in the shadow of a brother, I was discovering the one my parents had hidden from me. And I didn't like him. Louise had painted a portrait of a seductive child, very sure of his power, identical to the one who crushed me every day. Fully aware of the horror of my desire, I would have loved to feed that image to the flames.

I HAD PUT off the moment of knowing for as long as I could, scratching myself on the barbed wire of a prison of silence. To avoid it I had invented myself a brother, unable to recognize the boy imprinted forever in my father's taciturn gaze. Thanks to Louise I learned that he had a face, the face of the little boy who'd been hidden from me yet had haunted me constantly. Permanently damaged by having abandoned him to his fate, and guilty of having built their happiness on his disappearance, my parents had kept him out of sight. I was being squashed by this inherited shame, much as I was beneath the body that ruled over mine each night.

I hadn't realized that it was he who my father saw beyond my narrow chest and spindly legs: that son, his sculptor's model, his interrupted dream. When I was born it was

Simon who they'd put once more into his arms, the dream of a child he could mold in his own image. It certainly wasn't me, a half-baked attempt at life, a rough sketch showing no familiar traits whatsoever. Had he been able to hide his disappointment from my mother, was he able to force a tender smile as he looked at me?

The whole family knew. They had all known Simon, all loved him. They could all remember his energy and confidence. And they had all hidden him from me. Without meaning to, they had wiped him off the list of deaths and also of lives, repeating what his murderers had done but out of love. You couldn't find his name on any gravestone, nobody spoke his name—nor that of Hannah, his mother. Simon and Hannah, obliterated twice over: by the hatred of their persecutors and the love of their family. Sucked into a void I couldn't approach without risking disaster. A shining silence, a dark sun that had not only swallowed his life but also covered all trace of our beginnings.

Simon. I was convinced I had walked later than him, said my first words months after he did. How could I compete? Troubled by the pleasure I derived from this failure, I turned it into morbid satisfaction: I surrendered to my brother, facedown on the mattress, his foot on my neck.

And it was Louise who had helped me meet him. Sooner or later his ghost was bound to appear in that breach, to loom out of the confidences we shared. My discovery of the little stuffed dog had brought him out of his darkness, and he had started haunting my childhood. Without my old friend I might never have found out. I would probably have continued to share my bed with that combative boy, not knowing it was Simon I was wrestling with, intertwining my legs with, my breath with, and always ending up defeated. I couldn't have known that one can never beat the dead.

IV

I ADDED SOME new pages to my tale as a result of Louise's revelations. A second story was born, the blanks filled out by my imagination—although this story could not efface the first. The two novels would coexist, lurking in the depths of my memory, each in its own way shedding light on my parents, Maxime and Tania, whom I had only just discovered.

Maxime marries Hannah on a beautiful summer's day under a peaceful, cloudless sky. After the registry office, they go to the synagogue. Joseph is delighted to be present at the wedding of the last of his three children. The bride's parents are also there, along with Robert, Hannah's brother, and his wife, Tania. They have finally met their brother-in-law Maxime, whose praises Hannah has so often sung in her letters. The very next day they will travel back to Lyons.

The parents of the bride have booked the back room of a brasserie near the Place de la République for the wedding lunch. The dishes keep arriving until it's time for the guests to shake off their torpor. A trio of musicians has been hired; the violins and accordion revive the party. On the polished dance floor dark suits clasp flowered dresses, the heat is forgotten, and they take off to the rhythm of the band. *Mazel tov!* Everyone toasts the young couple, a glass is wrapped in a napkin and smashed, and the strongest men lift the groom shoulder-high on his chair.

Maxime would have preferred to do without these traditional celebrations, but he participates with good grace. He has yielded to his in-laws' insistence and agreed to a religious wedding. Ever since adolescence he has done his best to shake off his origins, and does not enjoy being reminded of them. He makes himself join in, smiles at everyone, takes part in the ceremonies out of respect for his young wife and her family. Since his bar mitzvah, the important rite of passage he felt unable to deny Joseph, he has always avoided participating in religious celebrations. The only worship he has observed is that of his body; he has devoted all his free time to it. He can't imagine spending Friday night by candlelight, praying and sharing the traditional Shabbat meal with his family.

He is almost thirty years old. Marriage will, he hopes, mark the end of his frantic quest for sexual encounters. Easy conquests, bodies consumed in a single night, their charm fading in the early hours. He was attracted to Hannah's grace and vulnerability; her family's prosperity helped win him over. He has exhausted the pleasures of the bachelor life and for the first time feels the desire to be a father.

HANNAH'S PARENTS STEP out of their car; they open the back door for the young bride, who makes her appearance in front of the town hall wearing a transparent veil over her hair and carrying a bouquet of fresh flowers. Maxime comes toward them to greet her, top hat in hand. She looks at him. Her emotion is visible in the pallor of her cheeks and the slight trembling of her hands. Other cars are parked nearby, the guests are getting out, men in suits and women in jackets and skirts or pastel dresses.

Maxime keeps an eye out for the arrival of Robert and his wife, Tania. Hannah has often spoken of her brother, the young man with the cheeky smile. She has also confided her admiration for her sister-in-law, an accomplished athlete and outstanding swimmer and high-board diver.

They arrive. Robert is just as Hannah described, with short wavy hair and laughing eyes, but Tania is the most beautiful woman Maxime has ever seen. Tall, slender body in a flowered dress, cascade of black hair tied back with a narrow ribbon, dazzling smile.

His chest hurts. Such beauty is agony to him—far from brightening the party, it casts a terrible gloom: this young woman's radiance breaks his heart. This is his wedding day, the day he will join his life to Hannah's, and he is struck down by this summer lightning. He seeks out the gaze of the woman who is to become his wife and guides her over to the town hall. Deeply disturbed by Tania, he tries to reassure himself: it's probably just the dormant ladies' man within him having one last flutter. A few months earlier his desire would have swept any obstacle out of the way; he would have done anything, destroyed everything if necessary, to make this beauty his.

In the registry office, family and friends gather behind the young couple; a rustling crowd from which escapes the odd giggle or stifled sob. Maxime and Hannah exchange their vows, and kiss each other while everyone claps. They walk to the table to sign the register.

For Maxime these moments pass in a fog. He turns toward the gathering to smile at everyone. He shouldn't have looked for her face, knowing he would be dazzled once again. Tania is sitting next to her husband, looking down. For some seconds he stares at this woman, the sight of whom has changed everything. A simple look, an almost imperceptible intent, but with incalculable consequences. What if someone spotted that gaze? But the guests are entirely taken up with their own emotion, smiling and talking among themselves. He no longer sees anyone but Tania, forsakes the ceremony, forgets his family, his friends. He stares at the young woman so hard she hears his silent call and lifts her head. Her black curls slide over her dress, parting like a curtain to reveal her eyes. He holds her gaze for just a second too long. Then turns back to sign the register. He refuses to think how he is insulting Hannah, not to mention all those who have come to honor them.

A little later, as the deep voice of the cantor reverberates under the vaulted ceiling of the synagogue, he lifts his eyes to the balcony where the women are sitting. Tania is in the front row, her eyes cast down. The young woman has probably forgotten his first look. But he stares at her again. She opens her eyes, struck once more by a bolt of surprise.

Nothing else matters; the absurdity of his behavior makes his tribute even more impassioned. Everything is hanging in the balance. Tania is the most beautiful woman he has ever come across; he cannot allow her to escape without letting her know, with this lingering look.

In the restaurant, far enough away from her, Maxime will have time to pull himself together. He'll do justice to every dish, chat merrily with those sitting next to him. He'll dance with Hannah, with his mother-in-law, with most of the women present, but will avoid this closeness to Tania, to her body under the flimsy fabric of her dress, the smell of her neck, the brush of her hair. When at last the guests depart he will feel great relief: Tania and her husband are returning to Lyons, and he doesn't know when he will see them again. The sight of his sister-in-law almost ruined his wedding; he and Hannah are about to share their first night together, he must not think of anything else.

Later that night, holding his young wife's body in his arms, Maxime will battle not to grasp Tania's curls in his hands, or take her mouth into his.

MAXIME AND HANNAH have been married for a few months. Maxime does sometimes think of Tania, whom he hasn't seen since the day of his wedding, but Hannah is enough to fill his life. He works in his father's shop; his wife joins him on Mondays, their busiest day, when the retailers come to get their supplies. The rest of the time she contemplates her growing belly. The child they yearn for will arrive in the spring. They live in a small flat on the avenue Gambetta, with a balcony overlooking the Père Lachaise Cemetery. Every Sunday Hannah accompanies Maxime to the sports club. She's a respectable tennis partner, and spends the rest of the time sitting on the lawn knitting or reading under the shade of the tall trees.

Simon is born at the beginning of spring, sturdy and yelling at the top of his lungs. They give him Joseph as a middle name. When the doctor holds him up by his hands to test head control, Maxime imagines his son on the rings. He enjoys seeing himself in the line of his son's eyebrows, in his determined chin. A new life begins for the three of them. Simon develops faultlessly; he sleeps well, has a ravenous appetite, and smiles at everyone. He has eight years left to live.

A few months later Robert and Tania come to visit. Maxime feels anxious before their arrival but is soon re-assured. Still just as gorgeous, Tania is very natural with him and wide-eyed about the baby. An afternoon spent beside Simon's cradle is enough to stop him idolizing her. His son claims all his attention, makes everything else fade into the background. Hannah laughs at the teasing of her brother, who seems happy and often puts his arm around Tania—though Maxime does notice that her belly is still flat.

On Sundays Hannah puts Simon in a Moses basket and settles under a chestnut tree between the tennis courts and the gym. Maxime comes over from time to time, glistening with sweat, a towel around his neck, to stroke his son's cheek and kiss his wife before disappearing again. He can't

wait to initiate Simon into all these disciplines, intro-
ducing him to the wrestling mat or grabbing him by the
waist to lift him to the chinning bar.

Simon also knew the shop on the rue du Bourg-l'Abbé.
He too climbed the stairs, ran along the corridors,
explored the stockroom. He probably built shelters out of
the empty cardboard boxes littering every room, just as I
did. He played at working the till, helped serve the customers . . . I'd been repeating his actions without knowing
it. He'd drunk the same hot chocolate in Louise's rooms,
sharing his worries and dreams. If he had any worries, that
is. Unlike me, he wasn't plagued by a body that constantly
betrayed him, wasn't deceiving himself when he read
admiration in his father's eyes.

Simon lived a carefree early life—Louise told me so,
giving substance to his little ghost—until the day menace
knocked at their door on the avenue Gambetta.

The threat of war is drawing near. Maxime and Hannah's
lives are governed by the events turning Europe upside
down. Joseph is glued to the radio, he reads all the newspapers. The harassment he was subjected to in Romania
sent him into exile; he is more attentive than others to

the dark cloud spreading over neighboring countries. Maxime keeps telling him that they are in France, land of freedom, and that nothing comparable could possibly occur. He doesn't like the gleam of fear in Joseph's eyes, can't bear to see his shoulders droop; sometimes he is sharp with his father, mocking him for his worries.

Simon is of course kept out of these discussions, sheltered from the darkness. He is loved, surrounded with tender care. He is protected, people on the street smile at him; how could such a world change and turn hostile? How could these kindly adults one day become his persecutors, jostling him and shoving him into a truck full of straw, separating him from Hannah? The newspapers report armies gathering in nearby countries, magazines publish photographs. When he catches a glimpse over his parents' shoulders of these impeccable troops, the flares, the banners flapping over crowds in dress uniform, he is astounded and his eyes open wide.

DAY AFTER DAY, during our afternoons together, Louise helped me turn the pages of a book I had never yet held in my hands. I entered with her into the upheaval she and my parents had experienced. She would fill her glass of liqueur to the brim, and smoke each cigarette so hard she almost burned her fingers. When the bell rang to announce a client she would sigh, stand up reluctantly, and ask me to wait. She would rush the appointment and return to take up her story once more, to flesh out my own.

Austria is annexed and Poland invaded, and France enters the war. The pages turn: victory of Nazi Germany, signature of the armistice, establishment of the Vichy regime. Names ring out, shouted in the street by newspaper sellers; faces are displayed to which France will entrust her fate. Tanks parade and troops goose-step down the Champs-Elysées. A man in full foreign regalia stands on the flat roof of the Trocadero, his hands clasped behind him, looking at the Eiffel Tower as if he owned it. The evil spreads; in just a few months good and bad become confused, and previously familiar figures become danger incarnate. Individuals who used to ensure law and order, control the traffic, or stamp official papers are now the zealous lackeys of an intransigent plan, functionaries whose mere signature can shatter a life. The enemy can no longer simply be distinguished by gray-green uniforms and long raincoats; it may also be hidden beneath the shiny cuffs of local government employees or the capes of policemen, the authority of police chiefs, or even the friendly gaze of one's neighbors. The big platform buses that took city dwellers to work and dropped passengers at parks and cinemas will soon become heavy with cargoes of men and women loaded with bundles of belongings. The small buses that used to take excited families on their holidays now stop in front of buildings in the early hours, sowing terror.

One day Maxime arrives to find Joseph leaning on the counter, his face haggard. The shop's packer, Gaston, has just accompanied Timo, the Yugoslavian employee of the neighboring wholesaler, to the Japy gym, where the young man had been summoned. Gaston has come back alone, instructed to return with a few personal effects for his friend. Word has been going around about these early arrests; the poor wretches will be held in places like Japy, transformed into assembly centers. Joseph sees in this the early signs of a persecution that will become much more extensive. He knows, and has told anyone who will listen, that what he fled from in Romania is going to repeat itself. Already Germany's Crystal Night and then the legalization of inferior status for Jews have led him to anticipate the worst. But his family doesn't want to hear. Word in the neighborhood is of raids becoming widespread. Maxime tries once more to reassure his father: Timo is being harassed not because of his Jewish origins, but because he has foreign papers. They know from the newspapers and radio that the purification policy aims to deport all those who have not been naturalized. Joseph and his family have been French for decades; what would they have to fear?

Maxime is burying his head in the sand. The anxiety of the neighbors irritates him, he doesn't care for their tearfulness, their wringing hands; he greets these fearful people coldly, and is sometimes brusque when showing them out. He still wants to believe in the impossible. Like many others he has heard tales of abduction in the small hours and knows of the drives to purge the country of undesirable elements. But he continues to believe that these measures are aimed at Poles, Hungarians, Czechs . . . stateless refugees who barely speak French, Orthodox believers who haven't changed their lifestyles and have thus created a ghetto in the heart of Paris.

He is, however, aware that the threat is drawing closer. This threat is personified by the man Germany has elected to power. He can't rid his mind of the sinister figure whose cries of rage have led him to hate the language that until that point had soothed him with its Lieder and operas, nurtured him with its literature and philosophy.

The pages are turning faster and faster, the images becoming increasingly sharp. The lines, the housewives waiting a whole morning to pay a fortune for poor-quality meat, a few previously disdained vegetables, or some bread that will have to be sliced as thin as possible. But most important, Joseph's direst predictions are shown to be correct when men are seen picking up hastily tied bundles and cramming themselves into buses under the orders of the French police.

Later, disbelieving eyes will witness these same black-and-white images of sealed wagon doors, and the fog of stations from which there is no return.

MAXIME HAS REFUSED to go to the police station to have the defamatory red mark stamped on his identity papers. This decision is the cause of much family conflict. Esther and George have made themselves known, Elise and Marcel are still holding out, Joseph is waiting on his son's decision. They all debate the subject heatedly.

Maxime trains with new energy: building his muscles has become a stand against cowardice and submission. He has never won as often, nor beaten his opponents so easily. He is keen to cover his chest with medals, to stand on the highest step of the podium. He takes Hannah and Simon to the club every Sunday; the little boy is his father's pride and joy, his agile body excels at balancing exercises, sequences, and somersaults. He will soon start apparatus work and wrestling.

★   ★   ★

Robert, younger than Maxime, has been called up to the Eastern front. Tania took care of the Lyons shop for as long as she could, but difficulties caused by the slow arrival of supplies and the closing of factories finally forced her to close the doors. She has returned to Paris and her mother's house in the rue Berthe. Loneliness has made her draw closer to her husband's family; she sees Hannah and Maxime regularly. The problems she dealt with in Lyons and the panic she feels each morning as she opens the post have left their marks on her face. She looks haggard, and takes less trouble with her appearance than she used to, but she has only to smile or move a certain way for Maxime to be just as dazzled as before.

One Sunday Louise, George, Esther, and Tania accompany Simon and his parents to the club to check on the boy's progress. They'll have lunch on the banks of the Marne, feasting on fried fish and white wine, and in the afternoon Simon will show off his talents. If she wishes, Tania can take up her training again. When she appears after lunch in her tight black swimsuit, Maxime realizes the real reason for his invitation: he wanted to see her in that outfit. He thought he'd transcended this painful feeling at the back of his throat; once again, as on his wedding day, he is bowled over by the sight of her. Tania dives off the high board, tracing a perfect shape and then disappearing beneath the water. Maxime can't take his eyes off the line of those shoulders, that waist, those finely chiseled legs.

Hannah claps, and then seeks out Maxime's tender gaze. All she sees in his eyes is Tania. She knows her husband well enough to recognize boiling desire, a fascination he is not even bothering to hide. He has never looked at her that way. She turns toward Esther and George: all these eyes shining for Tania with a similar intensity. She finds support only in Louise, who has understood and tries to reassure her with a smile. She sways; through a fog she hears the bravos cheering some new feat of Tania's. As her sister-in-law climbs out of the pool and shakes her thick hair, Hannah suddenly realizes what a perfect couple this sportsman and -woman would make. They are in their element, the place belongs to them, they are radiant. She is sure that George and Esther are thinking the same thing. Her temperament has never been competitive; she immediately wants to disappear, to obliterate herself, to make way for them. The day becomes gloomy and she spends the rest of the afternoon with Simon, hugging and kissing him, closer than ever to her son.

★ ★ ★

Esther and Tania have become friends, and light up the Sunday dinners with their laughter, banishing all threats. Hannah slips into the shadow of these two women with whom she could never compete. She disappears behind Esther's incessant chat and cheerfulness, bows down before Tania's triumphant beauty. Beaten, she takes refuge in Simon.

Their daily life is constrained by hardship, but brightened by the dinners organized by Esther with the little she has. All of them together around the table, forbidding themselves, just for the evening, from discussing current difficulties, leaving the darkness at the door.

WEARING THE STAR has become compulsory. A slap in the face for Maxime, who no longer has any argument for those he had tried to reassure. Joseph's concerns and the neighboring shopkeepers' fears were justified. The prospect of wearing the yellow badge annihilates all his effort, forcibly associating him with a community from which he would rather stand apart. Worse, the enemy is no longer the foreign invader but his own country, lumping him in with the unwanted. Once again, he decides not to obey; this scrap of cloth won't dirty his expensive suits, nor humiliate his wife and child. The tension in the family becomes highly charged. George reproaches him for what he sees as repudiation—he and Esther will wear the star with pride; why should they be ashamed? Every discussion turns into a row. Joseph hardly dares speak to his son, although he does occasionally try to make him see the danger in which this decision puts his wife and son. Maxime angrily sweeps these arguments aside: nothing distinguishes him to the enemy, so why should he be harassed? Does he have the aquiline nose, the clawlike fingers, or the receding chin of the posters shown to Parisians at the dreadful Berlitz Palace exhibition to help them recognize France's enemies?

Louise has complied, she has sewn the badge to her chest. She didn't have the strength to hide herself, but the star weighs on her, even more heavily than the chunky sole of her orthopedic shoe. Maxime drops by to see her every day, talks with her, asks her view of the situation. He is tempted to reproach his friend for surrendering, but her haggard face dissuades him. No further recoil is possible— as a wrestler he knows how an opponent will take advantage of a moment of hesitation, a flinching gaze, an uncertain move. It is time to cross the demarcation line with Hannah and Simon. He discusses this repeatedly with Louise. At first she tries to dissuade him, terrified by the risks, but faced with his determination she ends up proffering a suggestion: one of her cousins works in local government at Saint-Gaultier, a small town in the Indre; she will make contact to organize a place for them there.

Maxime is convinced that traveling into Free France is the only possible solution. The following Sunday he convenes a family meeting at George's place to canvass everyone's opinion. Elise, protected by Marcel's surname, favors staying in Paris; contact with political friends is her lifeblood; she is planning to help create a resistance network. George and Esther declare themselves ready, for different reasons: he has had enough of all the hardship, whereas to her it seems like a romantic adventure. But they both think it sensible to send the men, who are under the most threat, as a kind of vanguard. Once they are safe they can send word to the others. Simon will travel in the second group, with his mother. Tania doesn't want to abandon Martha, who would suffer with her so far away. The women would look after the shop and then, along with Louise, make the journey to Saint-Gaultier themselves. Everybody decides to take a week to think about it.

Is Simon aware, during this time, of the worry in everyone's eyes? He eavesdrops, hears talk of leaving; he must feel his father's helplessness and his mother's anxiety. But he remains at the epicenter of this little constellation. Just like his father, he knows how to get what he wants with a smile; he has the world at his feet. In the street he bumps into neighbors and strangers wearing this star on their chest; he wants one himself. Perhaps he even asked Hannah to sew one onto his jacket so that he could sport it proudly, like his father's medals.

TANIA IS BACK in the room where she grew up, in the rue Berthe. Her mother's sewing work provides them both with a relatively comfortable life. She has become used to the situation. Robert is no longer constantly on her mind, her hands no longer shake when she opens the post. She has received a few cheerful letters: he's not complaining, has been lucky enough to avoid the most dreadful front lines, assures her of his love, and tells her they'll have a child as soon as he gets back.

During her time in Lyons, Tania's life was limited to the bed shop and their small first-floor flat, and brightened only by her trips to the swimming pool. Robert was an attentive husband but lacked the imagination to break the monotony of provincial life. Her husband's childish personality started to weigh on her, and his blind compliance with his parents' wishes became unbearable: it was Robert's submissiveness that had resulted in their move to Lyons, and she couldn't forgive her parents-in-law for this exile. She missed Martha during that frightening time, and would have given anything to get back to her mother, the studio on the rue Berthe, and the busyness of Montmartre.

Back in Paris, she takes up with her family again. She enjoys the Sunday evening dinners at George and Esther's house. Esther has become a friend and confidante. She was glad to see Robert's sister Hannah again, and get to know her husband and their son, Simon—such a charming, imperious little boy, so like his father.

She can't deny an attraction to Maxime, whose looks seduced her the first time they met. But the lingering look he gave her on his wedding day made her blood run cold. She could see he was confident of his appeal, used to easy conquests, one of those men for whom women are prey.

Robert was proud to have married a woman who turned heads in the street, and had never stopped wanting her with the gluttony of a small boy. At the beginning of their life in Lyons they sometimes went down to the shop in the evenings and made love on one of the beds for sale. Robert would choose: rustic, seventeenth-century, or contemporary—the showroom displayed many kinds of bedroom, each promising different pleasures. The shutters were closed for the night but allowed light from the street-lamps to filter in; Tania, in her husband's embrace, jumped at every click of heels on the pavement.

She thinks about Maxime more than she would like. Try as she might to stop it, his image haunts her, the disturbing image of a man she doesn't love. Every time she sees him with Hannah and Simon she remembers that look. In any other circumstance she would have considered it simply flattering, but on his wedding day! She hasn't mentioned it to Robert or to Esther, and hates herself for this silence, as if it seals a pact between her and Maxime, this man she should despise but in fact desires. For the first time she is attracted to someone she neither likes nor admires. She is bombarded with precise images: his tanned neck against a white shirt, the shape of his shoulders, the prominent veins of his forearms. She lets herself go, imagining his smell, the weight of his body, his penis, the muscles of his buttocks.

With Robert she always called the shots, laughing at his impatience and playing with his desire. With Maxime, she knows she is already conquered; the feeling is new and unnerving. To get him out of her mind she takes up drawing again. She reopens her sketchbooks and on page after page takes possession of this body, emphasizes its shape, draws out the strength of its lines. The results surprise her by their contrast to the fluid figures she used to send in to the magazine every week. Thanks to Maxime she discovers in her strokes a strength and style she didn't know she had. This activity soothes her; she spends hours shut away in her bedroom, pencil in hand. Then, like a guilty child, she hides her sketches in the back of a drawer.

In the early summer an opportunity arises. The Lyons shop has become a useless burden, increasingly at risk of plunder. A buyer has appeared; could she meet with him and negotiate terms? Her mother-in-law, sorely afflicted by the conscription of her son, doesn't feel strong enough to make the journey. One of their friends who works at police headquarters could get her the necessary papers; she could use her English-sounding maiden name. Tania hesitates. Robert would have obeyed his mother without a word, but she needs time to reflect.

A possibility decides her: if her family-in-law accomplishes its plans and takes refuge in the Indre, she could join them once she has fulfilled her mission. She could spend this difficult time surrounded by people she loved, could share Hannah and Simon's life, she and Esther would become even closer. She would see Maxime every day.

THE DECISION IS made. Louise has been able to contact her cousin, who has given them the address of a retired colonel and his daughter who are willing to put them up in their house on the banks of the river Creuse. George and Maxime will cross the line first, and establish themselves in Saint-Gaultier. Esther, Louise, Hannah, and Simon will join them as soon as possible. Joseph does not want to risk it; crossing another border seems to him impossible. He will live in Malakoff with Elise and Marcel.

Finding a guide was not as hard as they had feared—Elise's friends gave them an address. The man met in a Belleville café inspires trust; he has crossed the line several times and swears they will be totally safe. They are to meet him in a village just south of Montoire; Marcel will drop them there. They know the conditions: a tidy sum to pay, very few belongings, savings sewn into the linings of their jackets, false papers.

Everything happens as planned: a date, a time, a quick drink in the back room of a café, and then a rustling moonlit walk through unknown countryside. The guard-house silhouetted against the starry sky, the anxiety of the crossing, and at last freedom. The handshake of the man before he slips back into the darkness, abandoning them on the outskirts of a sleeping village. Waiting for dawn in a straw-strewn barn, then the bus journey to Châteauroux. Finally a telephone call to the colonel, who comes to collect them in his ancient front-wheel drive and takes them back to his house. His daughter, Therese, shows them around. They are free; as soon as they've got their bearings they can send word to the women.

The little town nestles around its Romanesque church, perched on a steep slope overlooking the Creuse. Near-vertical alleys lead down to the weed-covered riverbanks. The river rushes between the piers of a bridge whose three arches create perfect circles reflected in the current, and plunges beneath the hydroelectric plant that transforms the gray water into light. The town center is made up of modest dwellings not more than two storeys high; at the edges of town, on each bank of the river, a few imposing houses reign over shaded grounds. The colonel's property sits grandly among ancient trees, surrounded by a low wall with a wrought-iron gate giving on to the riverbank. Their host and his daughter occupy the ground floor; the four bedrooms of the first floor are at their disposal. Maxime and George choose the largest for themselves and their wives—Simon and Louise will have the other two.

It all seemed so easy that they don't quite realize the risks they have run. Maxime takes Therese's advice and contacts the village school to offer his services, particularly with the children's physical education. George can look after the gardens and take up fishing again, to supply Therese with river fish to enhance their usual fare.

Therese—the village schoolteacher, now in her fifties—lives in the shadow of her father, the only man in her life. She runs the household with an iron hand, watching over the colonel's diet like a bossy housekeeper. This manless woman is suspicious of Maxime, but in the end the seducer brings her out of her shell. She shows her susceptibility to his charm with a thousand little gestures, and is at her window when he does his morning exercises shirtless on the lawn. She watches him, deeply moved, and confides this turmoil to her diary.

HANNAH LOOKS AFTER the shop on the rue du Bourg-l'Abbé, with Joseph's help. Esther is there too. Louise lends them a hand at busy periods, as her customers have become scarce; these days she sees only her most devoted patients, and would rather not think about why the others no longer require her services. The three women provide one another with support, confiding in one another and eating together. They've received a first letter from the men, singing the praises of Saint-Gaultier and promising to write soon to give them the green light. Simon reigns over the little group, and clings to his mother, who now has only him. Hannah feels so alone in the flat on the avenue Gambetta that she doesn't have the heart to stop her son coming into her icy double bed. He moves into his father's place, head on his pillow, clutching a stuffed dog: every night the little man becomes once more a fearful child, afraid of the shadows in his bedroom. Hannah watches him drift off, moved by his determination to fall asleep, seeing Maxime in those dark eyebrows and clenched fists. Maxime is her whole life, of this she's more sure than ever. In a few days she'll be with him again, sharing his warmth, his nights.

This woman, who trusts so easily and gives her love so freely, feels guilty for finding her sister-in-law a threat. Since that afternoon at the sports club, her heart is always on the alert. She admires Tania, but her vivid strength and untamed beauty are a danger and Hannah can't help feeling relieved when she goes back to Lyons. She thinks of Robert often, every day fearing bad news. She prays for her little brother to come back and for Tania once again to find refuge with him. She is proud of managing to run the business without her husband, happy to watch over Simon devotedly and deprive herself for his sake. Maxime will be grateful to her.

Poor Hannah. Those were the words that came to mind later, when I found photos of her. I was touched by her plumpness, by the freshness of her clear eyes shining at Maxime with complete trust. Eyes that would soon dull, a smile on which the heavens would soon fall. Until the second letter arrived she was able to believe that her departure for the other France would bring her renewed happiness. But one by one the walls she leaned against every day, so unsure of her own strength, came crashing down.

The operation has been kept secret. In the middle of the night the whole eleventh arrondissement is cordoned off; police are waiting at the end of every street and at every metro exit. Officers rap on doors, waking sleepy families, barely giving them time to pack a few things before jostling them down the stairs, sometimes with a kick or the aid of a rifle butt, and cramming them into buses. Where are they being taken? Nobody knows; the most optimistic have heard talk of a Jewish state that Hitler's Germany is intending to create somewhere in Eastern Europe, or perhaps Madagascar, and which will become the new Palestine. Others, those who are trying to escape, who are throwing themselves out of windows or hastily entrusting their children to the neighbors, don't believe that story for a moment. They know that beyond the French borders are places from which no one returns. As soon as Hannah arrives at the rue du Bourg-l'Abbé, Esther tells her the news that has been going around all the shops in the area:

the biggest raid since the start of the Occupation has just taken place. She rushes over to the boulevard Richard-Lenoir, and knows as soon as she sees the closed-up shop and flat. The doors have been sealed, and the neighbors confirm that early that morning her parents were taken away, along with hundreds of other inhabitants, registered or denounced.

The first wall has just come tumbling down. Hannah falters; she returns to the shop and throws herself into the arms of Esther and Louise. Through her sobs she calls for Maxime, like a lost child.

THE SECOND LETTER from the Indre brings Hannah new hope. The men write that everything is ready, and that the banks of the Creuse will help them forget danger and hardship. Then, struggling to decipher Maxime's cramped handwriting, she comes to two lines that hit her straight in the heart. The long-awaited letter falls from her hands. Tania has just joined her brothers-in-law; she arrived from Lyons a few days before and has moved in with them. Joyfully announcing the good news, Maxime writes that when the women and Simon arrive in Saint-Gaultier the family will be almost all together.

The second wall comes crashing down. Hannah left the protection of her family to take refuge under Maxime's wing; without him she is nothing. She feels as if she's losing her mind. Her parents have abandoned her and she's suddenly convinced that her husband is about to as well. She needs no proof—she knows instinctively why her sister-in-law has gone there. Deep inside her a certainty has established itself: nothing can prevent those two from being together. Tania is there, with Maxime. Everything has changed; life is suddenly unbearable. Esther and Louise watch her stagger; her legs give way, and white as a sheet, she clutches the counter. When they read the letter they both understand. Esther is deeply distressed by Hannah's pain, wishes she could tell her how responsible she feels. It was she who gave Tania the colonel's address just before she left for Lyons.

They decide to bring their departure forward. Gaston, the shop's packer, has obtained the false papers they need; they know the guide's contact details; in just a few days they will be in Saint-Gaultier. Hannah leaves all the organizing as well as the closing of the shop and Louise's consulting rooms to them. She doesn't respond to anything; they have to take her in hand, pick out the things she'll need, pack a bag for Simon. On the eve of their departure she suddenly refuses to go. She wants to stay in Paris with her son, needs to wait for her parents' return, if Robert comes back wounded she'll have to take care of him. Her eyes are all over the place, she's almost raving; it takes all Louise and Esther's strength to convince her. Thanks to their efforts she finally agrees to leave, but withdraws into total silence.

Marcel has taken charge of driving them toward Montoire and dropping them where they will meet the guide. Simon is excited by the adventure and stares out of the Citroën's windows at the passing countryside, making comments to his mother, who barely glances at him. Louise and Esther are also silent. Made vastly more anxious by Hannah's behavior, they dare not express any affection toward her for fear that she will burst into tears. She doesn't say a word until they are in the café. A bit later she will speak, for the first time since they left Paris. She will say a sentence, just one, and it will be the ruin of Simon.

Louise had given in to my pleas and told me things that would remain forever etched into my brain. She had told me all of it, everything my parents told her, everything she experienced alongside them. Except the most important thing. A shadowy area remained: the family wanted to believe it was Hannah's mind-blowing carelessness that led to her ruin, dragging Simon down with her. But I was so insistent that my old friend eventually told me what had really happened that evening in the café, right near the guardhouse. Timid, shy Hannah, the perfect mother, had turned into a tragic heroine; the fragile young woman suddenly became a Medea, sacrificing her child and her own life on the altar of her wounded heart.

ESTHER AND LOUISE are sitting at a table next to the bar. Hannah and Simon are farther away, near the window. The restaurant is empty; they are the only customers. A big grandfather clock ticks audibly. The landlord is wiping his counter and chatting with the guide. Everything seems totally calm, a foretaste of the freedom awaiting them only a few miles away. The man has advised them to split up so their group won't attract attention. After putting their bags in a shed outside, he brought them some drinks. He has checked the duty times, and knows at what exact moment the guards' attention will be distracted. He has told them that they will have to act fast, collect their bags and run through the darkness along a little path whose every stone he knows. Simon has been told that they're going to walk through the countryside at night; he hugs his stuffed dog and drinks the lemonade the man has brought him.

Hannah doesn't touch her cup. She is staring at the starry sky beyond the window; from time to time she absently strokes her son's hair. Esther and Louise watch her anxiously from the other side of the room. Simon says he wants to go to the toilet. He is shown the way. Hannah starts to get up but he waves her off—he is old enough to manage alone. As he passes he gives his dog to Louise to look after. She smiles as she watches the adorable, confident little man walk toward the back of the room.

The sudden squeal of car brakes. Footsteps ring out in the night, and three uniformed officers appear in the restaurant doorway. Louise and Esther feel themselves blanch. Louise instinctively hides the little dog under the table, then brings her hand to her chest to make sure no stray threads from the unstitched star still remain. Hannah doesn't react to the men's arrival. The guide's back stiffens; leaning on the bar he brings his glass to his lips and stares at the rows of bottles. Two of the men stand guard by the door. The third walks over to Louise and Esther and asks for their papers. They control the trembling of their hands and take their identity cards out of their bags. As Louise stands up, the thick sole of her orthopedic shoe bumps against the chair leg. The man says something in German to his colleagues; they reply, laughing. The landlord attempts a joke, the guide forces a smile. The officer doesn't respond, just stares into the eyes of the two women after he has had a good look at their photographs. He returns their papers, checks the guide's, and walks across to Hannah, who is still gazing out the window. When he is near her, he holds out a peremptory hand and the young woman looks deep into his eyes. Louise and Esther hold their breath; they see her rummage in her bag, look at her papers, put them on the table in full view, and then bring out others that she gives to the man, holding eye contact all the while.

Disconcerted, the officer raises his eyebrows. He glances at the document, and immediately barks out an order. Esther and Louise, frozen, realize what has just happened. Then pattering on the floorboards. Simon has come out of the toilet and is rushing toward his mother. Louise would like to signal him to keep quiet and come to her instead, but it's too late. The man questions Hannah with his eyes. She doesn't hesitate; her voice calm, she replies: "My son."

Hannah and Simon are leaving the restaurant, flanked by the three men. It has all happened in a few seconds. Hannah is already far away, her eyes lost. Simon follows his mother, passing the women's table without saying a word. As he goes by Louise makes to stand up, but a firm hand on her shoulder—that of the guide, glaring—forces her back down. The officers haven't seen; the door closes on the dark night; in the restaurant they hear the car starting, and once again silence. Esther and Louise slump over but the guide gives them no time to think; he is pale, his forehead glistening with sweat: it's now or never. They must leave, collect their things from the shed, and take the path that leads to freedom; they will carry with them the bags that belong to the woman and child. As she stands up, Louise brushes against something under the table: Simon's dog. The little boy has left without his friend. Giving it back to him would have condemned them, and anyway she didn't think of it. She presses it to her face, wetting it with her tears.

The man hurries them, rushing them out. Esther is a shocking sight: her black eyeliner has run, creating greenish rings under her eyes; her thick red hair emphasizes her pallor. The night is cold despite the time of year, and the sky studded with stars. Louise hugs the little dog to her chest, thinking that Simon was right to protect him with the coat Hannah had knitted.

★ ★ ★

An hour later they are in unoccupied France. The country-side is restless with murmurings, the long grass ripples with prowling cats, a bird of prey screeches. The women walk down a deserted road bathed in moonlight, looking for somewhere to shelter until daybreak. Louise imagines the pitiful sight the two of them must present: a pallid ghost, makeup streaming and choking back her sobs, alongside a pathetic limping Jewess with a bag in each hand and a stuffed dog under one arm. On the other side of the line a car drives through the night, headlights sweeping the hostile road. To what nightmare is it taking its passengers, a distraught woman and a small boy trying to penetrate the darkness with his anxious eyes? Louise and Esther's thoughts are identical: they have failed in the mission entrusted to them. How can they face their arrival at Saint-Gaultier, how will they break the news to the waiting men?

WHEN TANIA APPEARS at the gate to the grounds, Maxime is chopping the trunk of a tree blown over in the wind. He has found a rhythm, repeating his movement such that the blade sinks deeper each time into the cut. This activity occupies his mind, and stretches muscles that have been inactive for too long. George has not yet come back from fishing; he is sitting on the riverbank under a willow tree. His bucket is full of fish. He's imagining coming into the kitchen, and Therese's joy when she sees his loot. The colonel's daughter is sitting on a deck chair on the terrace, reading, soothed by the regular thud of the axe. From time to time she gazes lingeringly at the man in shirtsleeves, admiring his exertions and shouting a few words of encouragement.

It is she who sees Tania first. She jumps, startled by the beauty of the young woman standing stock-still on the other side of the low wall, a traveling bag in her hand. A perfect body in a short gray dress with tailored shoulders and a neat waist. She feels her heart contract; she is sure this radiant arrival augurs no good. The two men have talked about her, and she recognizes Tania even before Maxime looks up and sees her himself. He starts, leaves his axe wedged in the tree trunk, wipes his forehead. They are facing each other. Maxime, arms dangling, stands a few meters from Tania, who remains quite still behind the gate. Therese knows as soon as she sees the look that passes between them. A cloud crosses the sky and blocks the afternoon sun.

Tania moves into the twin-bedded room intended for Simon. Maxime and George fuss around their sister-in-law, showing her around the village, taking her to see the church and the priory, walking with her along the banks of the Creuse.

Soon after her arrival she tries to call her parents-in-law; but without success. She imagines the phone ringing in the empty living room, piercing a deathly silence. She sends a reassuring telegram to Martha, but doesn't want to think about Robert. Like a headstrong teenager she has given in to a whim; she is finally near the man she desires, more attracted to him than ever. She struggles against the temptation to take refuge in his arms, to glue her mouth to his. Nothing matters outside this force that has completely taken her over.

Day after day Maxime's gaze becomes more insistent. She looks back at him, lets herself be flooded by these waves of desire. She can still indulge in this dangerous game; Hannah and Simon's arrival will put an end to it. Every time she yields to Maxime's piercing gaze she is aware of Therese watching: the schoolteacher is reacting like a jealous child.

Maxime tosses and turns at night, thunderstruck by Tania, obsessed by images of the young woman sleeping in the next-door room, her hair spread out over the pillow, her tanned skin against the pale sheets.

AS SOON AS Esther and Louise arrived they collapsed into the arms of George and Maxime. Louise would tell me that neither of them felt strong enough to describe Hannah's suicidal act, so they spoke instead of carelessness, of a lapse.

What kind of life could they build in the shadow of Hannah and Simon's absence, which had left each prey to unbearable images? Maxime retreated to his bedroom, spending long hours sitting on the edge of the bed with his head in his hands. The bags brought by Louise and Esther had been put in a corner, behind an armchair; they would remain closed on their memories. The little dog with the knitted coat sat on Simon's bag, looking after its master's belongings. Maxime couldn't bear to see it, asked for it to be removed. His son and his wife in the hands of the enemy, no doubt herded with thousands of others into

116

one of those pens where hatred was given full rein. And he, shaded by the garden's great trees and soothed by birdsong, wholly absorbed in his desire.

I tried to imagine my mother's feelings when she heard the news: the enemy whose threat she had fled had become an ally, sweeping away the only obstacle between her and my father. It all became possible, if Hannah and Simon weren't coming back.

At Saint-Gaultier they try to reassure themselves. They want to believe mother and child are being detained in one of those places whose names will be forever tarnished: Drancy, Pithiviers, Beaune-la-Rolande. Horribly overcrowded and lacking the bare necessities, certainly, but surely one couldn't die there? Only the colonel knows better; his conversations with the Resistance network and the news he receives from his American contacts have informed him of absolute evil beyond the borders of France. He does not discuss this with any of his guests: he does not like to add to their worries, and still refuses to believe in an undertaking of such monumental destructiveness.

Maxime, shut in his bedroom for most of the day, draws a cloak of silence around himself. Nobody knows what to say to him; they honor his suffering. The absent figures of Hannah and Simon hang over everyone in the great house. They think they hear the little boy stampeding up and down the stairs; they would like to take him swimming in the Creuse. They imagine Hannah on the terrace, busy with her embroidery, gazing lovingly at her husband and child wrestling on the lawn. Tania is trying to keep away from Maxime, and spends her days with Esther and Louise. They walk the country paths, talking about anything and everything except Hannah and Simon. How could Tania continue to play with Maxime's desire? She avoids him, lowers her eyes when their paths cross. The absence of his wife and son erects an insurmountable barrier between them.

The weeks go by. Slowly Maxime returns to life, coming out of his room to chop wood for hours at a time, going off on long walks. They all watch him surreptitiously, searching for a spark of life in his lackluster eyes. When the house awakens the table is already set for breakfast, with fresh bread and jam ready: Maxime has been up since dawn and, after his morning exercises, has taken care of everything. He cannot linger in bed; as soon as he wakes anguish weighs heavily on him. The notion of a detour to Tania's room has become impossible; although he despises superstition he almost believes he has been struck by divine retribution. He goes to the post office every day to telephone Paris; when he comes back nobody dares talk to him.

In the early afternoon when the sun is at its hottest, Tania puts on a swimsuit with a light dress on top and walks down to the Creuse with a towel over her arm. She swims from one bank to the other until she is utterly worn out. She practices her diving from the pier of the ruined bridge. In the freezing water she stares at the undulating grasses and the grayish layer of sludge. A procession floats past her eyes: scraps of vegetation loosened by the current, then caught in the sluice gates. She emerges into the blinding light to gulp a lungful of air and shake out her hair as if to dispel a bad dream, then throws herself once more into this intractable swimming. She exhausts her body, leaving the water only when she is completely out of breath and her muscles are barely responding.

When they gather in the evenings, conversation is slow. Maxime takes his leave first—they listen to his heavy tread climbing the stairs, his bedroom door closing. A little later George and the women go up to bed. Before they drift into sleep, every one of them thinks of the missing two, huddled against each other in a night filled with tears.

NIGHTS SPENT SEARCHING for Hannah and Simon are driving Maxime to distraction; sometimes, remembering Louise and Esther's tale, he curses his wife's stupidity. How could she have left her real papers in the bottom of her bag? Thanks to her he may have lost his son.

As soon as he emerges from these weeks of isolation he seeks out Tania with his eyes. He no longer wishes to resist. One afternoon, while the household is dozing, he accompanies her to the river. Without a word they walk across the estate, pass through the gate leading to the river-bank, and spread their towels on the warm grass. Tania undresses in front of him, letting her dress fall to reveal the black swimsuit she wore at the sports club. She dives into the river immediately and starts her crossing, cutting through the water with regular strokes. Maxime watches her moving away from him, slicing through the glistening water. Half-way across she stops to climb onto the pier. She waves at him as the air shimmers around her. She stretches her arms, arches her back; he sees her thigh muscles tremble, and then she soars upward, staying suspended for a moment in midair. The sight of this black arrow silhouetted against the white sky reawakens his desire. The vise loosens and he weeps for the first time since Esther and Louise's arrival.

He doesn't try to hide from Tania; when she hauls herself on to the bank he shows her his agony, his naked eyes. She stands before him stock-still and dripping wet. She holds out a wet hand; he grabs it and buries his face in it. She comes closer and he puts his arms around her and presses his face against the fabric of her swimsuit. He is touching Tania's body at last. He has dreamed so often of lying down in her warmth, yet it's a swimmer's icy skin that is offered to him. The river water blends with his tears. They stay like that for a long moment, then pull away, still without a word. Tania lies down beside him and they both stare up at the sky. The town is sleeping, only the dull rumbling of the factory disturbs the silence. Maxime knows he will resist no longer.

When night comes he opens the bedroom door, creeps in soundlessly, slips between the sheets, and clings to the body of the young woman. Pain overwhelms him. His mouth against Tania's, the salty taste of his tears . . . he pushes against her, feels his muscles come to life, throbs against the young woman's belly. He doesn't risk a single caress, just clings to her body, wrapping his arms and legs around her. Intoxicated by the scent of her, he drifts into a dreamless sleep. For several nights they fall asleep like that, holding each other tightly, fending off the ghosts surrounding them. In the small hours he returns to his room as cautious as a schoolboy. The seducer has become a shy adolescent, seeking softness and tenderness from Tania, approaching her gently, satisfied with her kisses and the feel of her skin.

Finally, one night, he will permit himself to take her. Fear of being heard will curb his momentum. Louise, Esther, and George are only a thin wall away. Maxime will thrust back and forth, diving into the deepest part of Tania until the moment when, unable to hold back any longer, he will bite his lips so as not to cry out. The effort of controlling himself will make it ten times more pleasurable. He is holding in his arms the woman he has wanted for years, but as he falls toward sleep it is Hannah's face that comes to him. He pushes her away as hard as he can, driving her bright face back into the darkness.

THAT WAS AS far as I had got. With the help of Louise's revelations I had built this story, culminating in that night. A night during which a little boy and his mother finally left this world, to enter the silence; a night that sealed the destiny of my parents and would allow me to be born, a few years after Simon's death. I could be born only on this condition: his strength must make way for my frailty, he must disappear into the night that I might see the day. It was him or me, not so different from my nocturnal battles with the imaginary brother who shared my room. His name was never again mentioned, nor Hannah's; all that remained of them were some bags abandoned behind an armchair. Clothes, smells, a stuffed dog, some orphaned objects, and a few photos that would all be relegated to the shadows, and guilty thoughts, whose burden I would bear.

THE TENSION IS palpable at Saint-Gaultier. The household is on the alert, watching the lovers—in the evenings in the living room, at mealtimes in the dining room. Nobody is convinced by their apparent indifference. Esther can hardly contain herself; she would like to scream her contempt, to spit at the couple whose every embrace is an insult to the memory of those who have been lost. To her this is a crime, repeated night after night, banishing Hannah and Simon a little more each time. Louise tries to calm her but she too is torn apart, simultaneously indignant at Maxime's betrayal and inclined to indulgence. Unsettled by Tania's triumphant beauty, she accepts their togetherness as a natural fact against which it would be futile to fight. Therese suffers in silence, retreating into her usual mistrust of men: Maxime is just like the others, she should have realized that he's simply one of those from

124

whom she has protected herself, a male thinking only of his own pleasure. Her intuition was right; Tania's arrival did mark the end of a happy time. She treats her father harshly and, persnickety about the management of the household, bosses everyone around before going to her room as early as possible to fill the pages of her diary with bitterness. George and the colonel do not approve of the lovers' behavior but consider their union inevitable, the only way for Maxime to survive his pain.

What happened next? Did my mother and father, guilty in everyone's eyes yet overwhelmed by desire, dare to love each other openly, walking hand in hand along the banks of the Creuse, flaunting their liaison in front of the family? It probably happened gradually, minuscule gestures becoming bolder as time went by. I asked myself whether Esther had ever confronted my mother. I could well imagine my theatrical aunt screaming at her sister-in-law, giving in when she wept, falling into her arms, and eventually becoming her confidante.

The weeks passed, no doubt the disapproving looks lost their harshness, and life resumed—until the horror forced its way through the barrier of serenity that protected Saint-Gaultier.

The rumor starts making its way around town, in the shops, wherever people stop to talk. They can no longer keep their eyes closed, or believe that people are simply being displaced; talk is now of systematic extermination, of death camps. How can Maxime sleep once this news has entered the house, projecting onto the walls images of convoys, of barbed-wire fences? Hannah and Simon return to haunt his nights. He can no longer think they are being held prisoner on the other side of the demarcation line; he must now contemplate the worst.

I had to imagine the days that followed, until the end of the war. When we would know: Hannah's parents deported after the big raid, Robert's death from typhus fever in a stalag. One less obstacle for Maxime and Tania—the boy with the laughing eyes likewise swept away by history.

And we would eventually discover the destination of the convoy that had taken Hannah and Simon. The place needed a name. For the first time we would see pictures. Never would we forget the shadow of a gate silhouetted against a white sky, or the black rails leading to the abyss.

THE FAMILY IS back in Paris. The fate that beat down on Hannah and her relatives has left them safe and sound. Tania is living once more with Martha. Maxime couldn't bear the idea of sleeping in the avenue Gambetta flat, so he has set up a makeshift bed above the shop. The two lovers decide to keep apart; they no longer dare touch each other. It has become impossible to ward off images of those missing, impossible to love each other in these haunted places. They must wait.

When Tania learns of Robert's death she hardly mourns him; he is already so far away. She even thinks that at least she won't have to face him. But what if Hannah and Simon return from their exile? She tells Maxime, as soon as they return to Paris, that she will step aside. She has to say it, she wants to believe it. He listens to her in silence then hugs her tightly; they make themselves think of nothing.

After the Liberation, relatives are still hoping. In Paris they watch anxiously for arriving deportees, day after day going to find out what's happening, to read the lists posted in the foyer of the Hotel Lutetia. They move from group to group holding out photos; they ask questions, and wait for the buses to unload their cargo of ghosts onto the pavement.

Several times Maxime takes the metro to Sèvres-Babylone, and comes back distraught. A haggard mob floods into the reception rooms, their wretchedness standing out against the rich setting. Ghosts walking on the pile carpets, wandering among the great sofas and mirrors, swaying, leaning on the very bar where not long before German officers were making toasts to victory. Every child's face, every hollow eye and pale countenance startles Maxime. Beneath every woman's tattered clothes he thinks he recognizes Hannah's wasted body. An acute pain runs through him—hope, mixed with fear. A wall has gone up, muffling their voices—he struggles to remember tones, has forgotten the high voice of his son, his wife's murmurs. In vain he tries to bring back their laughs, their favorite words, their smell. He has begun the mourning process: Hannah and Simon will never come back.

It takes time for Tania and Maxime to be able to envisage a life together. Months of removing furniture, filling suitcases, picking up still-inhabited objects, folding clothes impregnated with familiar smells, clearing up. Maxime cannot bring himself to give away his son's toys; he puts them in the attic on the sixth floor of the building where he and Tania will live from now on. Which is where I found Si, when I went up there with my mother. Years before a real dog, Echo—a small black-and-white mongrel found on the banks of the Marne—came to share our lives.

I shall be born in that district, and live in that quiet street. One room of the flat will become a gym, where Tania and Maxime will train. They will marry, and work together in the rue du Bourg-l'Abbé, specializing in sportswear and becoming successful. On the other side of the corridor Louise will reopen her consulting rooms. They will go to the club every weekend. On Sunday evenings they'll attend the ritual dinner at Esther and George's house with the rest of the family. Their hurts will become less raw; only a dull pain will remain lurking inside each of them. They will no longer speak of the war, or mention the names of those who were lost. Shortly after my birth Maxime will once again cause tension by changing the spelling of our name. Grinberg will be washed clean of its *n* and *g,* those two letters that had become harbingers of death.

LOUISE HAD MADE it possible for me to piece together my guilty parents' romance. I was fifteen years old. I knew what had been hidden from me, and I in turn kept quiet, out of love. My friend's revelations not only made me stronger, they also transformed my nights: now that I knew his name I no longer wrestled with my brother.

I gradually grew away from my parents. Resigned myself to seeing cracks appear on those perfect beings. Watched them fight the first effects of age by redoubling their efforts on the courts each Sunday. My father suffered more than my mother; I sometimes glimpsed fear in his eyes when he looked in the mirror. One evening he came home crushed: for the first time a young woman had offered him her seat on the metro.

My appearance no longer caused me pain; I was filling out, my hollows were disappearing. Thanks to Louise my chest

133

had broadened, the hole in my solar plexus had vanished, as if the truth had until then been written there in hollows. I now knew what my father was looking for when he stared into the distance. I understood what silenced my mother. And yet I was no longer crushed under the weight of that silence, I carried it and it strengthened my shoulders. I did well in my studies. At last I could see respect in my father's eyes. Since I had been able to name them, the ghosts had loosened their grip: I was on my way to becoming a man.

A few years later my mother would lose her speech and the use of her legs as the result of a brain hemorrhage. I would watch her muscles melt away, and have to face the sight of this skinny, unrecognizable woman rocking back and forth in a chair. My father would be even more distressed than I. He was accustomed to fighting and would at first deal with the situation well, helping my mother with her rehabilitation. But the sight of his champion leaning on a crutch, her right leg swinging with every step she took, would soon became unbearable to him. Injured worse than anyone by this sight, he would decide to put an end to it.

ECHO HAD BEEN part of our lives for a few years. He spent his days with my father and slept on my bed at night. He had replaced Si, whose threadbare fur had been returned to the dusty memories of the attic: now that I knew what he had been through, there was no way I could face the flash of those little black eyes. How had my father been able to bear me hugging him to my chest and sitting him next to me at every meal? What about my mother—what had she felt, hearing once again the name I had snatched from the darkness, of the boy she must have always feared would reappear?

My father melted when he cuddled his black-and-white dog. He took Echo for walks in the woods, played with him as you would with a child, let him off the leash on Sundays at the club, rolled around with him on the grass.

Whenever I had time I would pass by the shop. As soon as I arrived I'd cross the corridor to visit Louise. We had never stopped talking. She still knew how to listen, looking deep into my eyes, breathing out great curls of smoke, her hands chasing away old hurts.

When I went back up to the attic to return Si to his bed of blankets, I came across a photograph album among a pile of magazines, barely visible under all the dust. Maxime and Hannah in their wedding clothes. I looked at my father in morning coat and top hat, saw for the first time the anxious face of his young wife, as white as her veil, looking at her husband with the pale eyes that would so soon fade to black. The stiff pages revealed family scenes, groups of strangers posing in front of sun-splashed houses, beaches, flower beds. A life in black-and-white, the smiles now gone; dead people with their arms around each other. At last I had seen Simon: photos of him filled several pages. His face seemed strangely familiar. I could see myself in those features, if not that body. A photo had come unstuck, and I slipped it in my pocket. It had a date written on the back and showed him in shorts and a vest, standing to attention in front of a field of corn, screwing up his eyes against the sun of his final summer.

ONE MORNING SHORTLY before my eighteenth birthday the phone rang. My father answered and then put the phone back down, staring into space, still touching the handset. He told us the news in a calm voice before leaning over to stroke Echo, who had come to lie at his feet. He remained bent down for a long time, tousling his dog's fur; when he finally straightened he went to put on his coat. He agreed when I asked to go too.

The neighbor who had helped Joseph with his shopping and housework let us in. On the oilskin-covered table I saw an empty plate, a half-full glass, and a crumpled napkin. I followed my father to the bedroom, where I was about to see my first dead body. Grandfather was lying in his bed, head thrown back, skin waxy, mouth open. My father looked at him, then turned to tell me that he was glad his father had died in his sleep. The best way of leaving this world, he added. I went up to Joseph's face and touched his cheek with the back of my hand. His skin was icy. What dream had carried him off? Had he known he was going?

We buried Joseph at Père Lachaise. We headed for the Jewish section, where my grandfather would be laid to rest next to his wife. I saw Caroline's grave for the first time, a stone's throw from Joseph's flat and only a few minutes' walk from the avenue Gambetta. Another question that I had never asked. When we used to walk around Paris my father often brought me to visit the famous dead of Père Lachaise, but we never took a detour around the Jewish section. Why would he pay his respects at the tombstone that bore his mother's name? He carried his dead inside him: those who had been dearest to him had no graves, their names marked no stone. More than once, when we passed the columbarium, he had told me of his wish to be cremated. Only now could I understand the real reason for his choice.

As soon as we arrived home my father picked up Echo and strode over to the French windows. He opened them and walked out on to the balcony, where he stood for quite a while looking down at the street, before shutting himself away in the gym as usual.

IN MY BACCALAUREATE oral exam I had drawn a card stating the subject on which I must speak. It was a name: Laval. Paralyzed, I had stammered a single sentence about collaboration. My examiner was not impressed. Convinced that I was talking to a Vichy sympathizer, I had gone mute, which cost me a repeat of my final year.

I chose to see this misadventure as a sign that I was still up against the brick wall. There remained a gap in my story, a chapter whose contents were not known even to my parents. I knew a way to unstick its pages: I had heard about a place in Paris where I could find the information I was missing.

At the Memorial of the Unknown Jewish Martyr in the heart of the Marais there was a documentation service; research by Beate and Serge Klarsfeld had made possible a complete census of every victim of the Nazis. By consulting the registers you could find the name of every deportee, the number and destination of the convoy in which they were deported, the date of their arrival in the camp, and, if they hadn't survived, the date of their death. I spent an afternoon there, leafing through volume after enormous volume. I finally found the names I was looking for among the thousands of others. Saw them written down for the first time. And learned their fate: Hannah and Simon had, after a spell in the Pithiviers transit camp, been dispatched to Poland, to Auschwitz. They were gassed the day after they arrived.

The number of their convoy, the date of their death: these were hard facts, figures. The events on which I had built my hypotheses became devastatingly real as I read the register. I kept rereading the names of those who had shared that terrible journey with Hannah and Simon, who like them had experienced the darkness of a sealed truck and the horrors of overcrowding. Names of men and women, names of children—whose deportation President Laval had authorized for the sake of family cohesion.

Knowing that they had been murdered on arrival some-how lightened the burden. That date put an end to all my fantasies. No more images of their years of imprisonment, their ordeals, their nights.

These things that I had just learned, my father did not know. What had he imagined of Hannah and Simon's captivity during all those years? What was he still imagining today, when he gazed into the distance or couldn't sleep? The turnaround troubled me: having been kept out of this tragedy for so long, I now knew more than my father about his secret. Should I leave him in his ignorance? For a long time I wondered, waiting for an opportunity that life would be sure to supply.

The following year I gained a distinction in my baccalaureate and decided to go to university. My discovery of psychoanalysis during the philosophy course had been a turning point. When, later, I was asked what had motivated my choice of subject, I would know what to reply: by being such a good listener, Louise had opened doors for me, helped me disperse the ghosts, given me back my own history. I now knew where I came from. Relieved of the load that had been weighing on my shoulders, I had turned it into strength, and would do the same with those who came to see me. At that point I didn't know I would be starting with my father.

ONE EVENING I returned from university to find my mother in tears. Echo had been run over. They had brought the little animal home and put him in the gym. Lowering her voice, my mother told me that since their return my father hadn't left their bedroom. She wasn't sure if he was reading or sleeping, and didn't dare disturb him. He hadn't wanted any lunch, and hadn't said a single word. He was probably feeling responsible for the accident: they had been walking Echo in the woods and my father hadn't thought it necessary to put him on the leash to cross one of the avenues. My mother added that she had never seen Maxime so distraught. My father had overcome the disappearance of his wife and son; the death of his dog was crushing him.

I went into the gym and bent over Echo, who had been laid on his side. His snout was all bloody. I could see my face reflected in his wide-open eyes. I suggested to my mother that I take him to the vet, who would know what to do with his remains. I carefully took off his collar, ruffled his fur one last time, and wrapped him in his towel.

I was back an hour later. I went into the bedroom; my father was sitting on the edge of the bed with his head in his hands. He had drawn the thick curtains, so the room was lit only by his bedside lamp. I sat down next to him and told him how sorry I was. He replied without raising his head, his voice dull. He told me that it was his fault Echo had died. I heard myself saying it was true, he was responsible—but only for that. The sentence just came out of my mouth. He sat up. I was staring at the window, my shoulder against his. His questioning gaze weighed on me. I added that I was proud of what I had inherited, proud of the challenge passed on to me by both of them, this still-open question that had served to make me stronger. Proud of my name, so proud I would like to reestablish the original spelling. This too slipped out and my father sighed, as if I were wiping out years of effort.

I took a deep breath and continued. I said Hannah's name, and Simon's. Overcoming my fear of hurting him, I told him everything I had found out, omitting only

Hannah's suicidal act. I felt him stiffen and clutch his knees. I saw his knuckles whiten, but, determined to continue, I told him the number of the convoy, the date his wife and son left for Auschwitz, and the date they died. I told him that they had not experienced the daily horrors of the camp. Only the hatred of the persecutors was to blame for the deaths of Hannah and Simon. Today's agony and his continued feelings of guilt served no purpose except to allow this hatred to produce ongoing effects. That was all I said. I stood up, drew back the thick curtains, opened the door, and asked my mother to come in. And I repeated the whole thing, so that she too would know.

My father left his bedroom to eat dinner with us. As I was going to bed, he stopped me with a light touch on the shoulder. I hugged him tightly, something I had never done. His body felt frail, the body of an old man I now towered over. Feeling strangely strong, I didn't shed a single tear; the death of our dog had provoked a new turnaround: I had just relieved my father of his secret.

Epilogue

ONE SUMMER EVENING I felt the urge to go back to the woods surrounding the castle near our house. I asked my daughter to come with me.

Rose and I walked up the road leading out of our village. We passed what had been the portcullis, and a bit farther on plunged into a tangle of branches and trees felled by storms, bringing us out at the back of the castle. Ensconced in the middle of its moat and flanked by four slate-topped turrets, it looked as if it were dozing behind its closed shutters.

Last time I had walked onto the estate by accident, and chance had led me toward the little cemetery. Who lay beneath those stones? Afraid of being seen, I had flinched every time a twig snapped. The silhouette of a gamekeeper on the castle esplanade had put me off going any closer.

But this evening the path was clear: we could step over the fallen tree barring entry to the grassy patch, and walk into the clearing where the graves were laid out.

In between I had done some research on the owner of the castle. An elderly villager had told me his name: the comte de Chambrun, a descendant of the marquis de Lafayette and a barrister specializing in international law. He had married Laval's daughter and become his father-in-law's fervent defender, and the author of various publications aiming to restore his good name.

Now I knew whose property we were on. My daughter and I approached the stone slabs. On the first we read:

Barye

1890

Pompée

1891

Madou

1908

Brutus

1909

A dog cemetery, similar to those that surround the old churches in our rural areas. A tradition established by the original owners and continued by their successors, to judge by the more recent gravestones:

Whisky

1948–1962

Son of Soko

My father's faithful friend

Josée de Chambrun

Vasco

1972–1982

Dying is the only sorrow

he ever caused us

Josée de Chambrun

"Faithful friend," "the only sorrow he ever caused us"; these commonplace expressions touched me. Echo flashed into my mind, abandoned on the table of a veterinary clinic to be incinerated with a mountain of other carcasses. But I soon started to feel uneasy as I read the tombstones, whose dates following fast on one another brought to mind the graves of children: Josée de Chambrun, Laval's daughter, buried her cosseted pets here.

His name had been pulled from the hat once again. President Laval, who in his defense hearing said that he had encouraged the deportation of children under sixteen so as not to separate families. Which is what I would have said in my oral, if that examiner hadn't struck me dumb with fear. I would even have added the appalling words of Brasillach: "Above all, don't forget the little ones."

How could the little ones be forgotten? They were ghosts without graves, smoke hovering over hostile lands. I stood motionless, staring at the inscriptions. It was in that cemetery, lovingly maintained by the daughter of the man who had given Simon a one-way ticket to the end of the world, that I had the idea for this book. The pain I had never been able to assuage by mourning would be laid to rest in its pages.

My daughter's voice startled me. She wanted to show me a slab a little way off, its top hewn into a semicircle, hidden by branches and more modest than the others:

Dear Grigri
1934–1948

This one had been particularly loved, and missed. Perhaps it was the brevity of the epitaph that made it so moving. But who had grieved for him? Once more the simple words touched me and I thought again of Echo—and then felt outrage. What to do with this anger? Desecrate the place, cover these stones with offensive graffiti? I felt bad; these thoughts weren't like me. Rose was showing signs of impatience, so I suggested she go back home to her mother and leave me here a little longer. She agreed and walked away, waving without looking back.

I sat down on a tree trunk. Behind me, as the sun began to set, the shadow of the tip of a turret stretched right down to the nearest tombstones. The only sounds were a rustling of leaves in the breeze and the sharp call of a blackbird. I looked at my hands resting on my thighs, the furrows that had gradually appeared there, the cracks. They reminded me of my father's hands, as I knew them in his final years. At last I resembled him.

I remembered Louise's hands, her powerful fingers soothing my parents. Esther's hands, flying birdlike around her face as she hosted the Sunday dinners. And finally my mother's hands, in the months following her attack, clenched around pieces of foam rubber so that her nails wouldn't dig into her palms. My mother, definitively silent, moving from living room to bedroom with the aid of her crutch. I relived my father's distress at this spectacle, his futile efforts to see in this figure the splendor of the woman he used to admire as she soared from the ruined bridge to hover in midair above the Creuse.

As I looked at the rows of tombstones in the grass I thought back to my father's final act. With his arm around his wife's waist, he had helped her stand up and gently walked her over to the living room balcony, for one last dive. What had he murmured in her ear before holding her close and diving with her?

LOUISE AND ESTHER, the only two surviving members of the family, accompanied me to Père Lachaise. The three of us kept vigil over my mother's coffin while my father, according to his wishes, was reunited with Hannah and Simon in a column of black smoke drifting out of the crematorium's chimneys. Together we collected his ashes and set them next to my mother, at her grave in the Jewish section. The two women tactfully stepped back to leave me alone at the grave. I saw them walking away down the tree-lined path, stooped and as distraught as after their crossing of the line. I rushed to catch up, slipped between them, and, arm in arm with my two old friends, walked with them to the cemetery gate.

Not long after that I returned to the Memorial of the Unknown Jewish Martyr, having read in the press that the Klarsfelds were planning to publish a book dedicated to the French children killed in the deportations. I gave the documentation service the photo of Simon I had kept in my desk drawer, along with the requested information. A few months later I received the heavy black book, that terrible album filled with smiles, Sunday clothes, and fussy hairstyles. There he was, screwing up his eyes in the sun with his wall of cornstalks behind him.

Many years after my brother had deserted my room, and after I had buried all those dear to me, I was finally giving Simon the tombstone to which he had never been entitled. He would sleep in there, with the children who had shared his fate, on the page bearing his photo, the dates of his short life, and his name, whose spelling was so like my own. This book would be his grave.

About the Author

PHILIPPE GRIMBERT is a psychoanalyst. He is the author of several works of nonfiction and a novel, *Paul's Little Dress*. *Memory* was awarded two of France's most prestigious literary prizes, voted for by readers—the Prix des Lectrices d'*Elle* and the Prix Goncourt des Lycéens—as well as the Prix Wizo, for the best work of Jewish interest in French literature. He lives in Paris.

POLLY MCLEAN grew up in Paris and Oxford. Previous translations include *Solibor*, by Jean Molla, and *Lobster*, by Guillaume Lecasble.